REWIND

A PINX VIDEO MYSTERY

MARSHALL THORNTON

KENMORE BOOKS

Published by Kenmore Books

Edited by Joan Martinelli

Cover design by Marshall Thornton

Images by 123rf stock

ISBN: 978-1098756291

First Edition

❀ Created with Vellum

ACKNOWLEDGMENTS

I would like to thank Joan Martinelli, Randy and Valerie Trumbull, Kevin E. Davis, Nathan Bay, Karen Sinclair, Lori Wallet, and Mark Jewkes and Louis Dumser.

1

WET. WARM. STICKY.

Groggy, very groggy. I remembered taking a sleeping pill. The ones my mother left when she visited at Thanksgiving. I took one because the guy I'd been kind of seeing, C.B., had come over for Valentine's Day and stayed the night. The first time we'd ever—really the first time *I'd* ever since my ex, Jeffer, died.

I didn't think I'd be able to sleep, so I took one. Or two. Sleeping pills. And I did. Sleep. Now, I was wet. Which brought up some very humiliating possibilities. Except it was mostly my back and side that were wet, so how could I have—

I struggled to sit up. Should I change the sheets? Wake C.B. up? What was it with these pills? They were super strong. Of course, I'd also had champagne. Two glasses? Three? Did it say something on the label about alcohol? Did I read the label?

Sitting on the edge of the bed, I looked down at my hand and saw that I was holding a bloody knife. That didn't make sense. Did these pills cause hallucinations? I had to be dreaming. I looked at the little Sony clock radio sitting on the unfinished wood plank that sat on a stack of bricks making a kind of headboard-slash-shelves thingy. 7:12.

C.B. wanted to get up soon.

I stood up. The knife fell out of my hand onto the floor.

That seemed real. Was real. I hadn't been dreaming. Had I? Was I? I turned around to C.B. planning to ask if he thought I was dream—

His side of the bed was soaked in…His eyes open, staring…

I began to scream like a girl. It seemed the thing to do. Then things began to move quickly. My downstairs neighbors, Marc and Louis, were at my door, knocking, then letting themselves in with the key they had. They rushed in, already dressed for the office in nicely pressed shirts and ties. Cologne in the air.

"Noah, what happened?" Louis asked, putting a hand on my shoulder. A hand that came away bloody.

"I don't know," I said, gasping for air. Screaming like that really takes it out of you. How do girls do it?

Marc looked into the bedroom. "Oh my God." Then he picked up my cordless and hit three buttons.

"Am I dreaming?" I asked.

"No dear, you're not dreaming," Louis said.

I was shaking. Shivering.

Marc was giving my address to the operator. "We don't know. We don't know what happened. He's just—he looks dead. There's a lot of blood."

"Why don't we sit you down?" Louis said, leading me over to the dining table next to the front door. Out my window I could see the thick layer of gray clouds hanging over the basin. It looked like it was going to be a dark, sad day in L.A.

As soon as I was seated, I said, "I want to take a shower."

"That's not a good idea."

"Louis, should we take his pajama top off, at least?"

"I don't think we should. We shouldn't disturb anything."

It began to hit me. My apartment was a crime scene. *I* was a crime scene.

The sirens began. Rampart Station was maybe a mile away, I heard sirens all the time. Normally, I didn't even think about them. But these, these were for me. Which gave them a whole different sound. They grew louder by the second.

Marc came over and handed the cordless to Louis, saying, "I

called the studio and left a message that I'm not coming in. You should probably—"

"Oh, yeah, you're right." Louis took the phone and stepped away.

"So? Who is he?" Marc asked, a little sheepishly.

"His name is Curtis Barry. C.B. He likes to be called C.B."

"And you have no idea what happened?"

"We went to sleep."

"I thought I heard a door shut and someone leave just before six. I thought, well, we knew you had a *date*. Small building, as you know. I thought your date left."

"No," I said. So that must be when it happened. Just before six.

The front door had been left open and a uniformed LAPD officer stuck his head in. "We got a call about a dead body?"

"Yes," Louis said. "Come in."

Two officers walked in. Both men. One black, one white. At that moment, they seemed enormous, their dark blue uniforms ringed with duty belts that held walkie-talkies, flashlights, mace, handcuffs, and black handguns in stiff leather holsters. The holsters had been unclipped and each officer had a hand on his gun. They made my small apartment seem even smaller.

"Where is the body?" asked the black officer. His name was Hood, according to the tag on his chest.

"In here," Louis said, leading Hood into my bedroom.

The other officer was named Farkas. He looked Marc and me over, determining if there was any danger. It was obvious there wasn't.

Almost immediately, Louis and Hood came out of the bedroom. Hood nodded his head at Farkas, who then went over to the bedroom door to survey the scene.

Hood took out his radio and said, "Possible one-eight-seven. Securing scene. Alert detectives, coroner—"

While Hood continued, Farkas came over to me and asked, "What's your name?"

"Noah. Noah Valentine."

"Can you tell me what happened, Noah?"

For a moment, I wondered why he picked me out to talk to first, but then I realized I was in pajamas and literally had blood on my hands.

"I don't know what happened. I was asleep."

"You slept while the man next to you died?"

It was on the tip of my tongue to say I'd taken a sleeping pill, but I remembered they were my mother's. I was pretty sure it was illegal for me to take them. Or even have them.

"We drank a lot of champagne," I told him, hoping that would cover it.

Farkas got out a pad and wrote that down.

"When did you wake up?"

"I don't know. Ten minutes ago—oh wait, I looked at the clock. It said 7:12."

"And you called your friends?"

"He started screaming," Louis said. "We live downstairs."

Turning to Marc and Louis, he asked, "Did either of you touch anything in the bedroom?"

"No. Noah was in the living room when we got here. We both looked into the bedroom but didn't touch anything. We didn't even go in."

"There's blood on your hand," he said to Louis.

"I touched Noah when we got here. On the shoulder."

Farkas nodded. Hood was off the radio and standing next to his partner.

"You two live downstairs," Hood said to Marc and Louis. It wasn't a question, they'd said as much.

"Yes."

"This is a small place and there are going to be a lot of people here really soon. If you could wait downstairs. The detectives will probably want to talk to you."

"I don't know if we should leave him alone," Marc said.

"Your friend will be fine," Hood said, corralling them out of the apartment. They looked back at me, worried.

Farkas took out a little notebook and asked, "Tell me, who is that in your bed?"

"His name is Curtis Barry," I said, again. "C.B."

"Have you been seeing him long?"

"No. Last night was the first time he ever stayed here."

"So you met him last night?"

"No. Um, we met around Thanksgiving."

Still writing, Farkas glanced up and gave me a curious look. I could tell he didn't believe me. Didn't believe that two gay men would wait ten whole weeks before having sex. I mean, we'd made out a bunch. Mostly in his car or my car. It was fun. It was like being in high school, if we hadn't been geeky gay kids. I explained none of that to Officer Farkas, though.

"And you have no idea who might have stabbed him?"

"No."

"You didn't hear anything?"

"No. I wish I had."

"You have no idea when he was killed?"

"Just before six o'clock."

"How do you know that?"

"Marc, who lives downstairs, he said he heard someone leave my apartment and go down the stairs around that time."

"So you think the killer walked out your front door? Do you think that's how they got in?"

"I don't know. Is the window open in there?"

Putting his notebook away, Farkas walked over and looked into the bedroom. "The window is shut."

"It was open when we went to sleep."

"It was fifty degrees out last night."

"I know. We're both from back East. We like it cold."

I mean, there was a blanket and a down comforter on the bed. And I wore pajamas. C.B. was naked, but he had said he was kind of like a furnace at night. I didn't really remember whether that was true or not since I took—

"There's a knife on the floor," Farkas said.

"It was in my hand when I woke up. I've never seen it before." I tried to remember what it looked like. It wasn't a kitchen knife. It was thick and curved. The blade was about four inches long.

The red-tiled walkway to my front door continued to the

corner of the building, creating a small balcony of sorts with a great view of the Los Angeles basin. Hood now stood out there with two detectives. I happened to know them both. One of them was Detective Brenda Wellesley. She didn't like me much and wasn't exactly subtle about it. The other was Detective Javier O'Shea. He liked me a lot, and also—at times—wasn't very subtle about it.

Wellesley was not a particularly well-kept woman. She wore her long brown hair pulled back in a messy ponytail, her clothes were rumpled, and her glasses had a habit of slipping down her nose. O'Shea on the other hand was, in my opinion at least, nearly perfect, with jet black hair, honey-colored skin, light brown eyes, and a jaw that was as square as a comic book super-hero. And, to make matters even more distracting, he was dressed in an expertly tailored chocolate brown suit. His tie was the color of cinnamon.

Farkas saw what I was looking at and went out to join them. The four of them spoke for a few minutes. Through the window, Javier glanced at me. I thought I saw hurt in his eyes, and concern, but mostly hurt. There was something between us, though exactly what I wasn't quite sure. He had a boyfriend, after all. And I, well, I had reasons.

Then, Wellesley came into my apartment, ignored me, and went right to my bedroom door. She looked inside and then quickly stepped back. Going back to the front door she said, "Make sure SID puts up biohazard tape. And everyone be very careful. This is a dangerous scene."

Then she turned to me and said, "His name is Curtis Barry?"

"Yes. C.B. He liked C.B."

"Why'd you kill him?"

"I didn't. I just, all I did was wake up. And there he was. Dead."

"You really expect me to believe you slept through a murder?"

"It's true," I said, weakly, knowing she'd never believe me unless I told her about the sleeping pills, and then she'd arrest me for possession. Being arrested wasn't going to make this day any better.

Javier came inside. He wore a pair of latex gloves the color of sour milk and carried a brown paper bag. "Brenda, before we go too far, I think we should collect his clothing."

"Now? One of the techs can do that."

"They're not here yet. I think I should do it."

"Where are you going to do it? The kitchen?"

"We'll just go into the bathroom."

"Really? That whole area—all right, suit yourself."

"Come on," he said to me. I followed him into my bedroom. He turned and asked, "Do you have something you can put on?"

My bedroom wasn't much bigger than my queen-sized bed, and had built-in closets along one wall and a built-in chest on another. Javier was pointing at the chest. I opened a couple of drawers and found myself a pair of gray sweatpants, a T-shirt and boxer briefs.

"So, you just want me to take off my pajamas and put them in the bag?" I held out my hand for the bag, expecting to go into the bathroom alone.

"I have to um—" He cleared his throat. "—watch. Chain of evidence."

"Oh."

"I could ask Wellesley to do it," he said.

"No," I said. I would have asked for someone else, but I couldn't think of any other possibility that wasn't even more mortifying than having Javier O'Shea watch me strip.

I walked into my little bathroom like I was walking to the gallows. Javier came in behind me. I set my clothes down on the toilet seat, turned around and looked up into his eyes. He looked away.

"You don't think I did this, do you?"

"You shouldn't say too much. It's the smart thing to do."

"But I didn't do this. You have to believe me."

He didn't respond. Instead, he took a funky looking gray camera out of his jacket pocket.

"Show me your hand."

"What is that?" I asked.

"It's a digital camera. Works with a little memory card. We have a reader back at the office that gets it into the computer. We're trying them out. Twenty-six hundred a camera so it's probably a nonstarter. Show me your hand."

I held out my hand.

"The other one. The bloody one."

I held out my other hand. There were two stripes of blood where the knife had lain there. Javier aimed the camera, pressed a button. It flashed.

"If you'd used that hand to kill someone there would be blood everywhere, not just on the knife and your palm. From the pattern, someone set the knife in your hand while you were sleeping. Turn around."

He took another picture. Then had me turn, again and again, raising my arms until he'd taken a photo of the front, back and both sides of my pajama top.

"You can take the top off now," he said, setting the camera on the edge of the sink.

I took it off and handed it to him. I stood there feeling scrawny and underdeveloped as he studied the flannel top. Self-consciously, I ran a hand through my hair, which probably looked—there was blood in my hair, dried blood, leaving my hand stuck. I eased it out.

Javier was done looking at the pajama top. He showed me the back.

"Oh my God," I said, shocked by how much blood there was.

"When you woke up, you were lying on your side?"

"Yes."

"It looks like you were on your side during the murder. See these sprays of blood, they probably happened while your friend was being stabbed."

I felt a little queasy and swallowed hard. "Uh-huh."

"Also, this thick bloodstain along one side. That supports your story. You told the officers you slept through this. The blood doesn't tell us whether you were asleep or not, but it does tell us that you were very still while the victim bled out. If you were on top of the victim stabbing him there would be blood all over the front of your pajamas."

I wanted him to stop, so I asked, "How do you know all this?

"I went to a lecture on blood spatter."

"Blood splatter? Is that what it sounds like?"

"Spatter, and yes."

"Well, lucky me."

He half-smiled. "Was he your boyfriend long?"

"He wasn't my boyfriend. I mean, he might have been eventually. Last night was the first time we'd…"

"So, how do you know him?"

"We met around Thanksgiving. We've been doing things. You know, dating I guess." I actually didn't want to tell Javier we'd met at Best Lives, a group for people with HIV and AIDS. I mean, if I thought about it I'd have known he was going to find out eventually, but I wasn't exactly thinking—

"I need the pajama bottoms," he said.

"Can I put a T-shirt on first?" Rather than stand there completely naked.

"Yeah. Oh no, wait." He took a quick photo of my torso.

"Why did you do that?"

"It shows that you're uninjured and that none of the blood is yours."

I didn't say anything, just pulled the T-shirt on—I'd gotten it over my head when I realized I'd made a horrible mistake. It was my *Murder, She Wrote* T-shirt. Marc and Louis' friend, Leon had gone to great lengths to get it from someone he knew at CBS so he could give it to me at Christmas. It had the name of the show in red, a large magnifying glass and a fingerprint.

When my head popped out, I looked up at Javier. He was frowning.

"It was a gift."

"Give me the bottoms."

I turned around and dropped my pajama bottoms. I wasn't

wearing any underwear. Since Javier was now looking at my ass I figured it was okay to ask a personal question.

"So, how's your boyfriend?"

"We broke up."

That was horrible news. Or great news. I couldn't decide which. I hadn't wanted Javier to know I was HIV positive, unsure of how he'd react, not wanting to be rejected for that—still, I couldn't help thinking that if he was single, we might have, could have spent Valentine's Day together and that would have worked out a whole lot better since I was pretty sure he wouldn't have gotten murdered while I was sleeping.

"I'm sorry," I said, to be nice.

"It's for the best."

Reaching over to the toilet, I grabbed my underpants and pulled them on—white, Calvin Klein boxer briefs, just like the ones Marky Mark wore in, like, a hundred magazines. Usually they made me feel sexy—just not right then. I grabbed my sweats and pulled them on as well. Thankfully, the show was over.

When I turned around, Javier had closed the paper bag and rolled the top down. He was using a black marker to write on the bag: 2-15-93, BARRY MURDER, NOAH VALENTINE PAJAMAS.

That was creepy.

He opened the bathroom door and we walked the few feet through my bedroom. C.B. was still there in bed. All alone. Someone had put a strip of red plastic across the door. It said, BIOHAZARD over and over again. We ducked beneath it.

In my living room were a couple of crime technicians in blue jumpsuits. Over their jumpsuits were dark windbreakers that said SID on the back. Wellesley was talking to them. She'd put a paper mask over her face, like the ones doctors wear. This was awful. The way she was acting. She didn't *know* that C.B. was HIV positive, that I was. But she was acting like she knew. Just because we were gay.

"What happens now?" I asked Javier.

"I don't know. I'm sure we'll need to ask you more questions. Eventually you'll write a statement. Why don't you have a seat at the table for now?"

As I sat down, I noticed there were more uniformed officers outside my window. That meant there were several black-and-whites downstairs in front of the building. One of them must have left their flashing lights on, because the little bit I could see of the building across the street was turning red on and off. And, with the front door open, I could hear the sound of a police radio drifting up from the street.

Then Wellesley saw my T-shirt. "You think this is funny? Do you? Do you think this is funny?"

"Um, no."

"Brenda, he just grabbed the wrong shirt."

"Gimme a fucking break."

"Can we—" Javier said, pulling her into my tiny kitchen. It was hardly private, but at first they kept their voices low so I couldn't exactly hear what they were saying. Then Wellesley raised her voice a bit, "Maybe he put his pajamas on backwards so it would look wrong. Did you think of that?"

"He'd have to know something about blood spatter. And it would take a lot of premeditation."

"You don't think this was premeditated? You know this guy, you know he's got a fascination with murder."

"That doesn't mean he's a murderer."

"I can hear you," I said, loudly.

A moment later they came out of the kitchen with glowering faces. Well, Javier was glowering. Wellesley was staring at me with angry eyes over her mask.

Javier stopped next to me. "Look, this is going to take most of the day, possibly longer. Do you think you can go downstairs with Marc and Louis?"

I nodded.

"Let's get whatever you need."

So then we went back under the biohazard tape into the bedroom. I got a duffle out of my closet. I grabbed a pair of jeans, a pullover sweater, a button-down shirt. Then I went over to the built-in chest and grabbed a T-shirt that didn't say

Murder, She Wrote on it, another pair of underwear, socks, my other pajamas. Then I went into my bathroom, Javier right behind me.

I opened my medicine cabinet and grabbed my AZT and dumped it into the duffle. Javier reached in and picked up the bottle. He read it. Of course, the bottle didn't say AZT, it said zidovudine. I wasn't sure he'd know—but then he looked up at me and I saw it in his eyes. He knew. He was silent for a moment, then said, "This is why—?"

I nodded.

"And C.B., he was…also?"

"I met him at Best Lives. Do you know what—"

"Yes, I do. It had something to do with the Rod Brusco murder."

"That's how I met C.B."

Javier shook his head, probably thinking about what Wellesley would make of that—hopefully thinking about that.

I reached back into the medicine cabinet and grabbed my Bactrim. Javier took it out of my hand, read it, then put it into my duffle. I took my daily multivitamins. Javier didn't look at them. Instead, he began nosing around the medicine cabinet.

"What are these?" he asked when he found my mother's Halcion and read the label. "Did you take one of these last night?"

I bit my lip.

"Don't answer that."

He dropped the Halcion into my duffle.

"Get it out of here."

2

"THERE'S ALCOHOL IN THIS COFFEE," I SAID, AFTER TAKING my first sip.

"Of course I put alcohol in your coffee. You woke up with a dead man," Louis said. I'd just taken a very quick shower, left a message at Pinx—the video store I owned—that I wouldn't be in, and had been telling Marc and Louis everything they'd missed. Or, most everything. It was just Kahlúa in the coffee, so it wasn't too strong.

Their apartment was just like mine, except it was decorated better. The living room had four armchairs that Marc had slip-covered in brown-and-black houndstooth, brown velvet drapes hanging from wrought iron rods, and a portable stereo sitting on a low shelf in front of the window.

We sat at the café table in their dining area. I could look directly into their tiny, U-shaped kitchen. Instead of the ordinary stove I had, Louis had installed an apartment-sized range, so there was enough room to fit a narrow dishwasher that could be rolled over to the sink when needed. The small stove just made it more impressive that he was able to pull so much good food out of such an itty-bitty kitchen.

Of course, his kitchen was well organized and overflowed into the dining area. There was a small rolling cart filled with pantry items standing next to the counter, a hanging basket for fruit, and a pot rack on the wall above the narrow stove. Ceramic frogs sat on the window sill over the sink, and a spice rack hung on the wall above that window.

"Javier gave me my mother's sleeping pills. I'm supposed to get rid of them. Do you think that's a good thing or a bad thing?"

Louis raised an eyebrow. "You can get arrested for having those."

"I know. That's why I didn't mention them to Wellesley."

"On the other hand," said Marc, "the pills explain how you stayed asleep while your friend was being—you know, stabbed to death."

"What are they again?" Louis asked.

"Halcion," I said.

"Ah!" he said. "You do know one of Halcion's side effects is murder?"

"What!?"

"Oh yes, they banned it in England for that reason. And there were a couple of cases here in the U.S. It was in *Newsweek*, I think."

"So if Wellesley found out, she'd be convinced I did it," I said, my stomaching churning. "I mean, more convinced."

"No matter what tall, dark and still *very* handsome thinks about the blood evidence. Yes, I think you're right."

"What should I do with them?"

"Give them to me," Louis said. I took them out of the duffle and handed them over. He opened the freezer and stuck them deep in the back.

"Isn't that an easy place to find them?"

"Only if they get a search warrant. And why would they be allowed to search our apartment?" A buzzer went off. "Oh, the scones are ready."

"Is that what smells so good?"

"We'll let them cool for a minute," Louis set the baking tray on the stove. "Now, let's go over this again. You and your friend went to sleep around midnight. Then, sometime this morning, someone got into your apartment through the open window in your bedroom?"

"And they left right before six," added Marc. "I heard a door shut and footsteps coming down the stairs."

"Are you sure it was a door?" Louis asked.

"It sounded like a door."

"The window was shut when I woke up," I said.

"Could the killer have climbed back through the window and shut it?" Louis asked.

"Maybe," Marc said. "But why shut it? Why not leave it open?"

"It won't stay open," I said. "I have to prop it open with a stick."

"So, they might have accidentally bumped the stick climbing out and the window slammed shut," Louis suggested.

"No, I don't think so."

I couldn't have slept through a window slamming shut a few feet away. Could I?

"Come on," Marc said, getting up. "Let's test this out." He started toward their bedroom. "Louis, you're the murderer. Go outside."

In their bedroom, a big cozy sleigh bed dominated the room. They'd shoved another dresser into the built-in closet and put a small TV/VCR combo on top of it. The door was open so they could watch TV. Marc walked around the bed to the window. He pushed aside the heavy drapes and said, "How open was the window?"

"A little more than a foot, maybe?"

"And there's no screen?"

"Only in the summer." I'd bought an expandable screen that I put in during summer when there were bugs. I watched as Marc opened the window to about the right height. Their window wasn't broken so it stayed where he left it. Outside, Louis took off their screen. I wondered if maybe I should spend more time calling the landlord and asking to get things fixed.

The window began about eighteen inches from the floor. Louis put one leg over the sill, crouched down as far as he could and tried to get into the bedroom. His back scraped against the bottom of the window. He stood up.

"Well, that was awkward."

"It was," Marc agreed. "Now go back out."

"Really?"

"Yes, you have to. You've just murdered someone."

Louis reversed the process, but this time, as he stepped completely out the window, he nearly fell down.

"There, see, he almost fell so he'd have let go of the window and it would have come crashing down. That's probably what I heard. Not a door, but the window."

"What on earth are you doing?" a voice asked from behind Louis. It was Leon.

A minute or so later, we were all back at the café table inside. Louis was putting a scone in front of me.

"So, Marc called and told me everything," Leon said. "I just have one question, and I don't mean this in a rude way, but why aren't you dead?"

Actually, it had crossed my mind as well. "I don't really know." I tried to butter my scone and kind of made a mess. Butter everywhere.

Louis put a scone in front of Leon and then put the rest in the kitchen. Marc scowled at him.

"Maybe we should back up," Louis said. "Whoever the killer is, they knew your friend, Mr. X."

"C.B.," I said, taking a bite of the wonderful, flaky, cinnamon scone.

"The killer knew he was staying the night at your apartment," he continued. "So, he's either someone C.B. told he was staying over or he's someone who was following C.B."

"And why didn't we know anything about this C.B. person?" Leon demanded. "You kept the whole romance a secret."

I decided to ignore that and asked, "Why aren't you two having scones?"

"We're on a diet," Marc moaned.

"We found this diet book from the sixties at St. Vincent

DePaul. *The Drinking Man's Diet*," Louis said. "It's amazing. It actually encourages drinking."

"It says wine has no carbohydrates, though even I don't believe that," Marc said.

"More coffee anyone?" Louis asked, holding up the bottle of Kahlúa. "No?" Before he set the bottle down he re-filled his cup. "Where were we? Oh yes, did your friend know he was staying at your house last night?"

"Kind of, I guess. I mean, we hadn't talked about it. But it was Valentine's Day and we went out to dinner. He took me to the Ivy so I asked him to drive, which meant he had to bring me home. And, yeah, I guess I kind of expected that he... and he just parked and came up."

"The Ivy," Leon said. "Did you see any movie stars?"

"No."

"Oh," he said, clearly disappointed. "Well, did you at least have the barbecued salad?"

"I did. I liked it."

"I think you were followed," Louis said.

"It's really hard to follow people in real life," I pointed out. "It's not like in the movies."

"Well, all the killer had to do was follow C.B. here, and then if he lost you, come back and wait."

That actually made sense.

"Did you see anything?"

I shook my head. "Could I have another scone? And some nonalcoholic coffee?"

"Well, did either of you notice anyone lurking about?" Leon asked Marc and Louis.

"No, but we were busy having our Valentine's Day," Marc said.

"You didn't go out?"

"Oh no, we stayed home and stayed on our diet," Louis said. "Steak and salad."

"And massive amounts of red wine," Marc added.

"And a little horizontal exercise."

"Louis, leave something to the imagination."

He shrugged and gave me another scone, then poured some hot coffee into my cup.

"I don't think you guys should stay on this diet for very long," I said. "You're going to end up in a twelve-step program."

They visibly shivered.

"All right," Leon said. "So, you two were lolling around in a drunken afterglow and didn't see anything. While you—" Meaning me. "—you came home with your boyfriend—"

"He wasn't my boyfriend. Last night was the first—"

"Whatever. What time did you get home?"

"It was around ten-thirty, I guess."

"Then you made the beast with two backs, and fell asleep around…?"

I was blushing and hating that I was blushing. "Midnight."

"And then the murder didn't happen until right before six," Marc said. I could tell he thought that was curious.

"Why did it take six hours for the killer to work up his nerve?" Leon wondered.

"Our next-door neighbors were up until almost three," Marc said.

"Really?" Louis asked.

"Yes. You put your earplugs in."

"Oooo, sexy," Leon purred.

"Maybe they fell asleep," I said. "The murderer, I mean, not the neighbors."

"I think waiting around to kill someone would keep me awake," Marc said.

"But you're not a killer," I said, "so we shouldn't judge a killer's behavior by yours. You're a normal person. A killer might actually fall asleep."

"Sunrise is around six-thirty."

"But it starts to get light earlier," I said.

"So that woke him up and he rushed up to kill Noah's boyfriend," Leon said, agreeing with me.

"Not—his name was C.B."

"Oh my God," Leon said. "Here's what happened: He was going to kill you too, but then decided not to because you didn't wake up. He stabbed—C.B.—and rather than kill you too, he thought he could pin C.B.'s murder on you."

That sounded very plausible. My life had been saved by two tiny sleeping pills.

A bit later we went out and sat in the courtyard so that Marc could smoke. His agreement with Louis, who didn't smoke, was that he not smoke in the house or in their cars. For that reason alone, they spent a lot of time in the courtyard.

Louis had purchased a secondhand standing metal heater from a rental company. It was about eight feet tall, worked on a gas burner at the top, and had a kind of metal hat that deflected the heat downward. It sat next to the table making a slight hissing noise.

Surrounded by tall banana plants and an enormous bird of paradise, we were sheltered from the wind. Still, it was only about sixty outside—even with the heater—so before we came out I snuck into the bathroom and put on my pullover sweater. It was black with six other colors woven in. I'd been thinking about throwing it out since was a bit too Bill Cosby for me. What I really wanted was a cashmere sweater I'd seen at The Broadway but hadn't been able to afford. For the moment, I was glad to have this sweater.

While putting it on, I took the opportunity to take my morning pills, then went out and joined the boys in the courtyard. When I got there, Javier was standing next to the table right under the heater. He had three clipboards and was handing them out to Louis and Marc, and had one for me.

"I need statements from all three of you. Basically the facts about last night: what time you went to bed, anything unusual you noticed, and then everything that happened this morning. You will be signing it at the bottom, so be as accurate as you can."

"How are things going upstairs? Have you found anything?" Leon asked, rather boldly I thought.

"I'm sorry, I can't share any details of the investigation," he said a bit too loudly. Then he lowered his voice and added, "We've dusted the bedroom window for prints and it appears it was wiped with a cloth that had some blood on it."

"A sleeve," Leon speculated.

"Possibly," Javier said.

"We think the killer planned to kill Noah too," Leon said, "but then changed his mind."

"Leon, you're just guessing. You don't have to tell him your guesses," I said, sitting down.

"It's not a guess. It's a theory."

"It's all right," Javier said. "The possibility had already occurred to me." Then he asked me, "Have you had any conflicts with anyone recently?"

"Me?" I asked.

"We shouldn't discount the possibility that you were the target."

"Noah!?" Leon said. "But if he were the target he'd be dead."

"Not necessarily. The killer could have decided his being accused of murder was a better outcome."

I shivered involuntarily.

"Well, that's an interesting theory. But then you *are* the professional, aren't you?" Leon said, practically batting his eyes.

"It's just a possibility." Javier smiled and added, "I'll come back in a bit for the statements."

We began to studiously work on writing our statements. Leon sat there impatiently. Louis finished first since he only had to write down that he'd heard my screams and came running.

"I think I should start lunch," he said, going back into the apartment. Marc and I continued with our statements.

Just then, two guys from the coroner's office came out of my apartment and descended the steps to the courtyard. Between them was a gurney with a body on it: C.B. It felt surreal; like something out of an Italian movie from the seventies. I couldn't believe our date was ending like this. It made no sense.

Marc stopped writing as well, and the four of us just stared as the coroners rolled the gurney over the red cement steps that led down to the street. Then a couple of uniformed officers left as well. It gave me the feeling things were winding down.

We looked at one another, then Marc said, "They'll figure out who did this."

"Or we will," Leon added.

"We should stay out of this as much as we can," I said, though I'd have been delusional if I really thought we would.

In a cloud of drugstore perfume, our new neighbor, Patty Wong, a fifty-something Asian-American woman with an effervescent personality, rushed over asking, "What happened?"

"A friend of mine died," I said, not really wanting to go into it.

"Oh, poor Noah! I'm so sorry. Was it a heart attack? I read about you boys, you know. The drugs, the sex!" She made a face that suggested jealousy more than condemnation. "You all need to be more careful."

"It was murder," I said. "He was stabbed."

Her eyes got really large. "Oh my God! Poor, poor Noah!"

"You didn't hear anything this morning, did you?" Marc asked.

"I heard some screaming. I thought the Mexicans were raping some poor senorita in the street." Which apparently didn't require a call to the police.

"Actually, that was me."

"Oh, poor poor—"

"Yes, I know, poor me."

She glanced at Leon and said, "Hello, Lee. How's tricks?"

"Excuse me, nature calls." He got up and hurried into Marc and Louis' apartment.

Patty claimed to know Lee—er, Leon from some long-past part of his life, but she wouldn't say exactly when or where. He, of course, insisted he had no idea what she was talking about and swore no one had ever, ever called him Lee.

"Well," Marc said, "we have to finish our police statements."

"Oh, am I going to have to do one?" Patty asked.

"Only if you saw or heard something."

She pouted. I tried to focus on my statement. I was pretty

much done. I'd written down everything that happened—except, of course, that I'd taken a sleeping pill. Or that Javier had told me to hide the remaining pills. I was almost ready to sign it.

Louis came out carrying an enormous salad on a platter. He saw our neighbor and said, "Well, hello Patty!"

"Oh Louis, that looks wonderful!"

"Thank you. I'm not sure there's enough—"

"You're so sweet to invite me!" He hadn't actually. "But I have to get back to work. Clients are waiting. That's the problem with working at home. You're never off the clock!"

"What is it you do again, Patty?"

"Ta! Let me know what happens! Such a tragedy!" Then she ran back to her apartment at the other end of the building.

Louis sat down with the salad and asked, "Have we figured out who her clients are?"

"One time I was doing the laundry," Marc said. The laundry was at the back of the building behind Patty Wong's apartment. "And thought I heard noises coming from her place. Sex noises. I think she does phone sex."

We all cringed.

"I don't know," Louis said. "She could be a pimp."

"What? No. Pimps need to beat people up," I said. "I mean, when it's called for."

"I meant for escorts. You know those ads in the back of the *LA Weekly*. She could be arranging dates."

"Should I get the wine?" Marc asked.

"Absolutely."

As Marc rushed into the apartment, Leon came out. When he got to the table he asked, "Is Patty Wrong gone?" He always called her Wrong instead of Wong. And I always kind of wondered if it was racist.

"You really need to pin her down and find out how she knows you," Louis said.

"She doesn't know me. She's just a nut job." Eying our lunch, he asked, "What kind of salad is that?"

"Romaine lettuce, grilled chicken, roasted tomatoes, Kalamata olives, feta, chilled asparagus. I made a raspberry vinaigrette."

"Sounds yummy."

"It feels weird, having lunch while the police are still upstairs," I said.

"It does," Louis agreed. "Do you think I should make them cookies later?"

"You can make me cookies later," Leon said.

Marc rushed back out with a magnum of inexpensive chardonnay and four glasses threaded through his fingers. Sitting down, he passed out the glasses and began pouring.

"That's a rather large bottle," Leon pointed out.

"There are no carbohydrates in wine."

"Oh God, you're still on that diet, aren't you?"

"It's working. I've lost five pounds."

"Or the scale broke," Louis added. "We're not sure which."

"Actually, the salad looks great," I said, trying to look on the bright side.

"So, Noah," Leon began.

"Oh God."

"It's time to shoot the elephant in the room. Tell us, who exactly was this C.B. person? How did you meet him? How long have you known him? Were you in love with him? Was he any good in bed? Everything. Tell us absolutely everything."

3

"WELL," I BEGAN AFTER A DEEP AND DEPRESSING SIGH. "Right after Thanksgiving I started going to meetings at Best Lives. And C.B. was always there, leading the group. He was, you know, friendly. I could tell—"

"Wait a minute," Leon said. "Best Lives is for—Oh, so you're HIV positive!? *That's* your big secret? Really, Noah, it's 1993. That's hardly a big secret."

I blushed horribly. "It was to me."

"Have some salad, *Lee*," Louis said, offering a plate.

"You're not funny, you know that don't you?"

"Noah, ignore them. Just continue," Marc said.

I took a deep breath and went on, "I didn't say much at first. I didn't really want to talk about the reason I was there. Other people talked. Their stories…" I stopped and took a sip of wine. "Their stories were kind of heartbreaking. There's a guy named Dante who's been positive since before there even was such a thing. He has no idea how he got it. All he knows is that when he got tested in eighty-six he was positive and, given his T-cell count, had been for a long time. He might have had ARC for a while, but now he's better."

"What is ARC again?" Marc asked.

"Aids-Related Complex. I think if you have only one opportunistic infection, then you've got ARC. Two is AIDS. But maybe not. They keep changing the definitions."

"And was Dante friends with C.B.?" Leon asked.

"C.B. was friends with everyone."

"Keep going," Louis said. "Don't mind us."

"There's this other guy named Michael. He looks like an accountant, but he was addicted to crack cocaine and then something called Tina, which I guess is cheaper than crack."

"Tina is methamphetamine," Leon said, earning looks from Marc and Louis. "What? I read."

"Anyway, Michael admits to trading sex for drugs, a lot, he thinks that's how he got the virus. And then there's Bartholomew. He's in his late forties, at least, and says he's been having sex since he was a teenager in the fifties. He has no idea where or when he picked up the virus, though at meetings he likes to tell stories about when he *might* have gotten it. Those stories are usually pretty dirty."

"You're supposed to be telling us about you and C.B.," Leon said.

"Sorry. I'd been to a couple of meetings and not said much. So afterward, C.B. came over and invited me to go out for coffee. I tried to say no, but he wouldn't let me. So we ended up at The Abbey, which was kind of a disaster since it was really loud and packed."

"Well, yes," Leon said. "Everyone's meeting their VGL SGMs there just to be safe."

"Another time, after a meeting, we went to the Formosa Café."

"Oh, I love that place," Marc said. "It's so old Hollywood."

"I know exactly what you mean," Leon agreed. "Every time I go there all I can think about is some sexy gangster beating the crap out of Lana Turner in the kitchen."

"Why would you think about something like that?" I asked.

Leon shrugged. "I don't know. I just do. Anyway, she looks fabulous through the whole thing."

I shook my head, sighed, and tried to continue. "Anyway, C.B. wanted to know why I didn't say much at the meetings. I explained that talking about myself was not my favorite thing."

I left a pause, expecting them to make comments about that. They didn't, though Leon did roll his eyes.

"Then he wanted me to tell him about how I seroconverted, so I told him—"

"Wait, what?" Marc asked.

"They don't," I started. "At Best Lives they don't say things like 'infected,' you know, they don't ask, 'When did you get infected?' They ask when you seroconverted."

"That's very clinical," Louis noted.

"But nonjudgmental. Anyway, I explained the whole Jeffer thing and then C.B. told me about how he'd been in musical theater. He was very proud of doing *Jesus Christ Superstar* at some theater down in Long Beach. And between shows he did temp work. They sent him to an advertising company in Santa Monica called Imagination Station. It was built in—"

"An old railroad station," Marc said. "I know exactly who they are. They worked on the *Minty* campaign with us."

"So, C.B. found out he was really good at advertising. They offered him a job and he decided to take it. It was a lot of money and I guess, well, he says he went a little crazy for a while. Lots of drugs and booze and boys. That's when he seroconverted. He said it was ironic because at Imagination Station he'd worked on one of the first safe-sex poster campaigns."

"Knowing better and doing better are two different things," Louis said.

"After he found out he was positive, he left advertising to work with Best Lives. I mean, he said he still did some freelance work, but mostly he just worked for Best Lives. And that was practically volunteer."

"Is there going to be any sex at all in this story?"

"Leon, stop interrupting," Louis said.

"I'm not interrupting, I'm prompting."

Louis mock-glared at him.

"Our first kiss was New Year's Eve," I admitted. "Bartholomew had a party at his apartment in Hollywood Hills.

It was a really nice party. He has a great view. There were a lot of people there and it was midnight."

"Romantic," Marc said.

I smiled. Taking a sip of wine, I continued, "Anyway, after that we started seeing each other a little more seriously. Dinner, movies, making out—he wanted to take it slow, I mean, we both did."

"And you kept it all secret from us," Leon pointed out.

"If it didn't work out, you'd tease me. And I just couldn't—"

"Did the guys at Best Lives know?" Louis asked.

"They figured it out. It kind of bothered a couple of them."

"Is there a rule against dating?"

"No. I think they wanted to go out with C.B. themselves."

"Jealousy is certainly a good motive," Louis pointed out.

"So, between New Year's and Valentine's you dilly-dallied," Leon said. "And then last night you finally decided to dally. How was it? Was it good?"

"I'm not telling you that."

"Don't want to speak ill of the dead?"

"Leon, it's none of your business."

"How can you be such a prude? You rent gay porn for a living."

"I rent videos—"

Just then, we heard someone on the stairs and saw that Javier was on his way down. In one hand he held a small gray case, similar to a fishing tackle box.

"Have you finished the statements?" he asked, setting the case on the table.

I hadn't quite. Taking a quick bite of salad, I hurried to finish up the last paragraph.

'We're all set," Louis said.

Javier collected their statements, then I gave him mine. He glanced at them each for a moment, like a school teacher who knew his students were subpar, and then set them down on the table.

Opening the case, he said, "I need to collect fingerprint samples. We're picking up a lot of prints so we'll need to eliminate everyone who's been in the apartment recently. If you could first fill out the top of the card."

He handed out three cards.

Leon asked, "Don't I get one?"

"Were you in the apartment this morning or recently?"

"Of course not. I don't know what you're implying."

"We don't need your prints."

"Oh. Well that's disappointing."

"What should we put under Reason For Fingerprinting?" Louis asked. He was moving along quickly. I was still putting in my height and weight. Since I was giving the card to Javier, I added five pounds.

"Just put elimination."

Leon was smirking, so I asked, "Don't you usually do this at the station?"

"When you tell people to come by the station to be finger-printed you'd be surprised at the number of people who just coincidentally forget."

"Done," Marc said, holding up his card.

"Okay," Javier said, taking an ink pad out of the tackle box. He came around the table, took the card from Marc and laid it flat. Then he opened the ink pad, took Marc's hand and began to roll his fingers, one at a time, into the ink, then onto the card.

"Do you have any idea when you'll be done?" I asked.

"You probably won't have access to your apartment until sometime tomorrow."

"It takes you that long to clean up?" Leon asked.

"We don't clean up."

"Oh."

Well, that was a terrible thought. One I tried to put out of my mind. Done with Marc, Javier came over to me and held out his hand for mine. There was something intimate about what he was doing, one man holding another man's hand.

Softly, he said, "Wellesley wants to search your car and Pinx."

"My store?"

"Yes."

"There's nothing there."

"Make her get a warrant. Otherwise, she'll just go in and take your computers."

"She can't do that. That's my business. We'd have to close."

"Will she be able to get a warrant?" Louis asked.

"Hard to say. She'll try to do it behind my back. She'll say that Noah's being found in bed with the victim is enough probable cause. But if the judge asks why he hasn't already been charged, she'll have to tell him that we disagree about the evidence. In which case, the judge might want to talk to me."

Javier was done with my fingerprints. He handed me a Wet Wipe to clean up. It wasn't all that effective, my fingertips remained gray. Javier moved on to Louis.

"I'm confused about something," Leon said. "What are you and Wellesley disagreeing about?"

"The blood patterns show that Noah couldn't have killed C.B.," Louis answered for Javier, who thanked him.

"Well, it doesn't sound like there's a lot to disagree about."

"I don't think she'd agree with you—"

And then, Detective Wellesley was standing behind Javier. In one hand, she held a plastic bag with the knife I'd found in my hand that morning inside. She waved it at me.

"Can you tell me where you bought this?"

"I didn't—"

"Don't say anything else, Noah," Louis said. "It's not a good idea.

And, honestly, I had to agree.

That evening, Marc and Louis went off *The Drinking Man's Diet* in order to have comfort food with me. Leon had left around five that afternoon, standing abruptly and announcing, "Well, I have a date. And I need a little time to get ready."

Then, to our shocked faces he said, "What? It's a Monday

night." That made no sense. Monday was not a date night, but we ignored that and said our good-byes.

By the time the police left completely, it had begun to get cold and dark so we went inside. Louis busied himself in the kitchen, while Marc and I sat in the living room drinking white wine. I felt pretty boozy, red-faced and fuzzy, which probably was the best thing for me.

"I noticed that Javier didn't say good-bye," Marc said. "Was he upset that you were seeing someone?"

"Tall, dark and gorgeous has a boyfriend, doesn't he?" Louis asked from the kitchen.

"Not anymore," I called out. "But I think he didn't say good-bye because I'm not talking to the police anymore. Right? I mean, he is a policeman, so…"

"Oh, I suppose that's true," Marc said. He leaned forward and with the sincerity that only comes after a bottle of wine said, "You know everything's going to be okay, right? I mean, you didn't do anything and you've got Detective O'Shea on your side. He knows you're innocent."

"I know. I'm mostly afraid they'll get a search warrant and take the computers from the store."

I really wished he hadn't mentioned that possibility. It had been nerve-wracking enough when I'd had to worry something might happen to the store during the riots. But at least then I could have put in an insurance claim. I was ninety-nine percent certain my insurance did not cover equipment taken in a police raid.

"Louis! Do we know any lawyers?"

"A couple. I don't know if they can do anything about a search warrant, though. I think that comes later. If there's not enough probable cause the warrant gets thrown out and so does whatever they've found."

"How does he know so much?" I asked Marc.

"*L.A. Law.* Speaking of which, did you see it last week? There's this stalker plotline that's just really creepy. Wait a minute. Did C.B. say anything about having a stalker? That could be what happened. People have stalkers a lot now."

"He never said anything." But was that right? Someone had to have followed him here. Does that mean he was being stalked?

"Louis! Do you remember that girl, the actress who got killed by a stalker?"

"*My Sister Sam.*"

"That's not her name."

"I don't remember her name," Louis said, coming around the corner carrying a cutting board packed with cheese and crackers. He set it on the circular coffee table the chairs gathered around.

"Crackers! We can't have crackers," Marc said. To me he added, "We can only have cheese and wine."

"I think we can suspend the diet. Just for tonight."

"Great idea," Marc said, reaching for a cracker. Skipping the cheese altogether, he popped it into his mouth. Then another. "Oh my God, carbs."

"How long have you been on this diet?" I asked.

"Two weeks. Two horrible weeks."

Louis frowned. "It hasn't been that bad."

A bit later he brought out the main course. It was a bubbling cheesy casserole.

"What is it?" I asked.

"Comfort food. It's mashed potatoes, three kinds of cheese, peas, garlic, chicken breast, some gravy."

I tried to think up an excuse to slip into the bathroom and take my meds, but after that afternoon I realized I didn't have to. Everyone knew. And nothing had happened. Nothing was different. Or at least not yet.

I got my pills out of my duffle and took them with the glass of milk Louis had set down next to my plate. Then I dished out a big pile of mashed potatoes.

"This is amazing," I said, taking my first bite. My appetite had come back after giving me a bit of trouble when I started on AZT. And this dinner was perfect. Mashed potatoes didn't really fix anything, but they did make things a tiny bit better.

During dinner, it seemed like Marc and Louis were deliberately talking about nonmurder-related things. Louis made a few comments about a speech the president gave about lowering the deficit. But then Marc said, "You can't possibly think either of us are interested in that?"

He shrugged and said, "Clinton's still working on a way to let gays into the military."

"Okay, well that's a little more interesting. Although, why anyone wants to be in the military is beyond me."

"The uniforms are nice," Louis said. "Did you ever think about the military, Noah?"

"No. Never. I mean, I registered for the draft like I was supposed to. But, no."

"I was in the last drawing."

"You almost got drafted?" Marc said. "You never told me that."

"I had a low number too, so if the war had continued I would have been called up in 1973."

"What were you going to do?" I asked.

"I was going to show up dressed like Carmen Miranda."

"Oh, my very own Corporal Klinger."

"So, is it a good thing if they do let gays into the military?"

"Yes," Louis said. "The military is an employer and it sets a bad precedent if they're allowed to discriminate."

"All right, this is getting boring too," Marc said, reaching out to take a second helping of mashed potatoes. "Have you read anything that's actually interesting?"

"Spielberg's trying to shoot a movie in Auschwitz, but they told him no."

"Okay, that's interesting," Marc said. "Is it about aliens?"

"Aliens at Auschwitz? I don't think so."

"Maybe it's not interesting then."

After dinner, Marc set up the TV in the living room so we could watch *Evening Shade* and *Murphy Brown*. There were a couple of movies we could have watched: one was about a plane crash in the Arctic and the other was about two drug addicts married to each other. I suppose it was comforting that other people had problems every bit as challenging as mine, but I still thought it was better to watch something that had a joke approximately every forty-five seconds.

We moved the chairs around so we all could see the TV and Marc brought out some extra blankets. To save time later, he also brought out the air mattress and began blowing it up while the show started.

"I can help with that," I said.

"I'm fine," Marc gasped.

Louis told me, "It's his penance for smoking."

That got him a dirty look. During the show, Marc took a break from his inflating duties, but when the commercial came on he began huffing and puffing again.

Meanwhile, Louis asked, "Why last night?"

"What do you mean?"

"Well, I assume C.B. has his own bedroom window. The killer could have crawled through his window on Saturday night or tonight or tomorrow. So, why last night? Why when he was with you?"

"Do you think—he planned to—implicate Noah?" Marc asked between breaths.

"No," I said. "It was too haphazard, too sloppy."

"You think leaving you alive was an improvisation?" Louis asked.

I hadn't really thought about it but, "Yes, definitely."

"So if the original plan was to kill you both, the police wouldn't have known which one of you was the intended target. They would have looked into you extensively."

"Or—" Marc said. "If the motive was—jealousy— last night— was the perfect time." The show was back on. He stopped blowing up the mattress. "We'll talk about this later."

Louis leaned over from his armchair and whispered, "You're handling all of this very well."

"I am?"

"Most people would be a basket case."

"I was a basket case. You heard me screaming."

"Shhhhh," Marc hissed.

Louis ignored him. "That was twelve hours ago. Most people would still be screaming."

We settled down and watched the show. When the next commercial came on, Louis said, "Oh, I've got something to help you sleep."

"I don't want to take any more sleeping pills."

"It's better than that!" he said, running into the bedroom.

"Do you know what he's talking about?" I asked Marc, who'd gone back to blowing up the air mattress.

"I—" exhale "—never do."

Louis came out with a Taser in hand. It looked familiar.

"Is that the Taser I used on Wilma Wanderly's son?"

"It is. When I brought it back to the spy store the guy offered to deduct the cost of the rental from the price, which made it a pretty good deal. And you never know when a Taser might come in handy."

"I guess you don't."

"Keep it nearby. But try not to zap anyone we know."

"Especially— us," Marc added.

4

THE NEXT MORNING, MARC AND LOUIS HURRIED OFF TO work. On the blowup mattress, I pretended to be asleep. I'd slept too poorly to want to talk to anyone before ten. The air mattress was not even close to comfortable—I'd slipped off it a few times. Plus, Marc and Louis snored terribly. That was something I already knew since we slept with our windows open in the summer. Actually, I slept with my window open most of the year—or had. Now that a murderer had crawled through it I'll have to consider shutting it.

After they left, I drifted in and out of sleep for a while and then got up. They'd left a note on the café table. Louis had made me a fresh pot of coffee and there were the scones from the day before. Marc had left a clean towel on the back of the toilet for me. They were so nice, but I was so glad to be alone. I'd barely had a moment to myself since I woke up the day before.

C.B. was dead. I didn't quite know what to think about that. I mean, I didn't know him very well. I'd wanted to get to know him, and I was sad that now I wasn't going to. But, I mean, the point was I didn't know him. Not really. So, other than the fact that it's never fun to wake up with a dead person, I didn't know how bad I should feel.

Angry. I *was* starting to feel angry. Someone had killed my date and was trying to blame it on me. Even though I'd said we should stay out of it, even though I knew we should stay out of it, I really couldn't. Staying out of it meant Wellesley would probably find a way to make me look guilty. I couldn't just stand around while that happened. I had a cup of coffee and a scone, took my pills, and wondered how, exactly, I was going to figure out who'd killed C.B. I had no idea.

After a quick shower followed by twenty minutes trying to dry my unruly hair with a blow dryer I barely understood, I packed up the remaining scones—they were definitely not on *The Drinking Man's Diet*, so I didn't feel bad about taking them —and left for Pinx.

My video store was a quick five-minute drive from my apartment. On Hyperion about a half block down from the Mayfair, the store was located in a small, bluish building made up of three storefronts. There was a dry cleaner on one side and a Taco Maria on the other. All three stores had big plate glass windows; mine was the one full of movie posters.

I parked in the back parking lot, which was sunken about five feet below street level. Walking over to the back door, I climbed the short flight of cement stairs and put my key into the lock. There wasn't much resistance; it was unlocked. Stepping inside, I reflexively glanced at the alarm panel, but it was not engaged. Or, at least, I thought it was not engaged. The alarm system I'd bought was confusing and the only thing I really fully understood about it was that when it went off—which it did on a regular basis— you had to get there quickly, put in the code, and turn it off.

Stepping into the store proper, I called out, "Hello?"

"Hi!" Mikey called back. Sitting behind the counter, he was in his mid-thirties, thin with brown hair clipped close to his scalp so that his bald patch wasn't as noticeable. He wore a white T-shirt with a black-and-white photo of two sailors kissing printed on the chest. Underneath it said READ MY LIPS.

"What are you doing here? It's Tuesday. Doesn't Missy work today?"

"No, she's taking that class on Tuesdays and Thursdays. So, now I'm off Wednesdays and Fridays. Remember?"

"Oh, okay. Well, why are you here so early? You don't have to be here for another forty-five minutes."

"I just wanted to get a head start. It's okay though. I'm not clocking in until ten."

"No, that's not okay. If you're working I have to pay you." We'd gone over this many times. He refused to understand.

"I'll take a really long lunch. I promise."

He'd tried that one before. I knew he'd take his regular lunch and pretend he hadn't. I rolled my eyes and set the bag of scones on the counter.

"What are those?"

"Scones my friend Louis made."

"Oh yum," he said, opening the bag. "See, I would have missed these if I'd come in on time."

"I wouldn't have eaten four scones in forty-five minutes."

He shrugged, took a bite of scone, and with his mouth full, asked, "Hey, I heard there was some kind of commotion up your way. One of our customers was talking about it yesterday. Someone died?"

I smiled weakly. I was going to have to tell him. He'd find out eventually. Still, it would have been nice—

"Yeah, that was me."

"But, you didn't die. You're right here."

"No, it was—a friend. My Valentine's date—"

"Had a heart attack? Randy says holidays are the worst." Randy was Mikey's boyfriend who was a trauma nurse at the county hospital.

I took a deep breath and told the truth. "Stabbed. While I was sleeping."

"You woke up next to a dead man?!"

"I did."

"That's the beginning of *The Morning After*. You are *so* Jane Fonda."

Just once I'd like to be Jeff Bridges.

"So, what happened?" he asked.

"I don't know. I slept through it."

"You don't have a drinking problem, do you? Jane was a total alcoholic. Massive blackout issues. Do you have blackouts?"

"I'd had a couple glasses of champagne. I'm not really used to drinking." I decided it was a good idea to leave out the sleeping pill. He couldn't tell anyone if he didn't know.

"I had to have Missy come in to help yesterday. Since you weren't here. She wants Saturday night off in exchange. That would leave us with just Lainey. And we know if she's not with Missy her grandmother has a tendency to die."

Lainey hated working without Missy, which had led to her grandmother dying three times. We agreed she'd die again on Saturday.

"I tried to get Carl and Denny to come in, but they've got tickets to the Gay Men's Chorus. I'm scheduled for the day shift on Saturday. I can stay. It's really not a problem. Randy is working that night anyway."

"No, it *is* a problem," I said. "You can't work from ten in the morning to midnight."

"I don't mind."

"I'll figure it out. Don't worry."

I'd made a point of being the one to do the schedule. Mikey would have happily handled it. And as I walked back to my tiny office, I wondered if I shouldn't have let him. I might be better off if I only had to keep track of when I should be there.

After I sat down at my desk, I stared at the schedule for the week and realized the only solution was for me to be there most of the day on Saturday. It was a busy day. Mikey could handle things alone for the first few hours, but then he'd need help. And I was the only possibility.

This was not going well. I really needed to hire another person, but I couldn't guarantee them a full schedule. I just needed someone for fill-in. But who'd want a job like that?

Deciding to solve that later, I booted up my computer. There was something I had to do; something that I either shouldn't do at all or should have done a long time I go. I had to look up C.B.'s account. I knew he'd rented videos from us because he'd mentioned being in the store. Since there weren't a whole lot of other things to do at Pinx he had to be in our system.

I signed into our proprietary program and entered Curtis Barry in the customer field. Nothing. I tried again with C.B. Barry. It came up. There was his address and phone number, both of which I already knew. His credit card number; he had a VISA that would expire 9/95. And that was it. That was pretty much all the information we collected, other than a list of the films rented.

I scrolled down and began to look at those. He liked the big releases, like *Batman Returns, Sleepwalkers, Alien 3* and *Apocalyptic*. There weren't any classic movies—which would have been a strike against him if he were alive. He also rented a lot of porn. And not just porn but the edgier titles: *Leather Training Camp, Bound and Gagged* and *Nights in Black Leather*.

Now I was uncomfortable. I hadn't had any idea C.B. was interested in leather. He hadn't said anything about it. And honestly, even though I'd had fun with him on Valentine's, it would have made a really boring porno. It was so…I don't know, normal. I wondered what would have happened if he hadn't been killed? If we'd kept dating? Would I have woken up one morning tied to my bed wearing a leather harness? I'm not sure I'd have liked that.

The phone rang. I decided to let Mikey get it. It was a quarter of eleven, so it was probably someone calling to find out what time we opened.

Then I had a terrible thought. I hadn't looked C.B. up before I began dating him. I hadn't because it felt like I'd be invading his privacy. But now, looking at the titles, I probably wouldn't have gone out with him. And if I hadn't gone out with him then he wouldn't have been sleeping in my bed, and if he hadn't been sleeping in my bed—well, he might still have gotten murdered. It just would have happened somewhere else. Which would have been nice.

The intercom buzzer went off. Picking up the phone, I said, "Hello."

"Noah, your mother's on the phone."

"Oh, God," I said before clicking over. "Hi Mom. It's not Saturday."

"Goodness, Noah, I can call you on other days of the week if I want to."

"I suppose. So, you don't want anything in particular?"

"I just want to know how you are."

"Well, I'm fine. I'm just as fine as I was on Saturday." Yes, that was an enormous lie, but I really didn't want to tell her the truth. No one wants to tell their mother, 'Had a date this weekend, had sex, and then he was murdered.'

"How are *you* doing?" I asked.

"Oh, I'm just fine."

"Good, I'm glad to hear that. Anything exciting happen since Saturday? Three whole days ago."

"Well, Leon called me."

"What do you mean, Leon called you? Since when do you talk to him on the phone?"

"Oh we're good friends."

"*When* did you talk to him?"

"This morning. He called me the minute he got to his office."

"Oh shit."

"I thought you'd say that."

"I really didn't want you to know what's going on."

"Well, obviously," she said. "But we still need to talk about it. Do you need a lawyer? I can ask my lawyer friend if he knows anyone in Los Angeles."

She'd made a number of references to her lawyer friend since Thanksgiving. Every time I tried to find out more she evaded my questions.

"Speaking of things we don't talk about, what's your lawyer friend's name? You'll have to tell me if he's going to make a referral."

She gasped. "You *do* need a lawyer."

"I don't actually. At least not yet. Just in case, though, you should tell me his name."

"Oh, all right. Cotton. His first name is Preston but he prefers to be called Cotton."

"Like gym class?"

"I don't understand."

"In a boys' gym class they always call you by your last name." I already wasn't liking him. I moved on. "So his name is Preston Cotton?"

"Yes, it is."

"Criminal?"

"Noah, not all lawyers—"

"I meant his specialty."

"Oh. Family law, I think."

"Is he from the South? His name sounds like he should own a plantation."

"No, he's not from the South. He's a born and bred Michigander. And I don't think they even have plantations anymore. In the South, I mean. They've never had them here."

I was pretty sure she was right.

"You must feel horrible," she said, with the kind of sympathy only a mother can muster. The annoying kind that makes you teary-eyed and pissed off at the same time.

"I do feel awful."

"Were you in love?"

"We'd been dating, it was the first time—"

"Ah. Infatuation."

She was right, I suppose. And I hated it. I always thought of my mother as too sheltered to really understand these things. I missed that woman.

"And how did you sleep—"

"You left your sleeping pills, remember? I took one."

"Oh, I see. Well thank goodness. I imagine if you'd woken up you'd have been—"

"Can we talk about something else? The whole thing is sort of upsetting."

"Of course, what would you like to talk about?"

"I don't know. I don't care."

"I read that Wilma Wanderly is opening in Las Vegas soon. At Lucky Days."

"Oh yeah," I said. This wasn't exactly changing the subject. Wilma's son had killed a number of people and even waved a gun at me the prior summer. All over a dress that I eventually sold to Wilma to put on display in the lobby at Lucky Days. "Well, good for her."

"Cotton and I are talking about going," she said casually.

"To her show? In Las Vegas?"

"Yes dear, that's what we're talking about."

"Well, have a good time, I guess."

"We haven't decided yet. It might not happen."

Then something occurred to me. Something I should have thought of already but hadn't.

"Mom, I have to go."

"Really? Well, all right. If you need anything, you'll call me, right?"

"Of course," I said, though the real answer was probably not.

"Oh, and one more thing."

"What's that?"

"Tell Louis I found the mercado in Grand Rapids. I love it!"

"All right."

"I love you, dear."

"Uh-huh. I love you too."

Hanging up, I thought for a moment about how challenging family could be. I mean, you loved them but they managed to bother you in ways no one else could.

And that made me think about C.B. and his family. What had he said about them? I'd gotten the impression they weren't close. Did he actually say that? I couldn't remember. I was pretty sure though that he'd grown up in San Diego.

I dialed long distance information, the area code for San Diego and the number 555-1212. It took about thirty seconds to find out there were more than a hundred listings for people with the last name Barry.

I was about to hang up when I took a chance and asked, "What about Curtis Barry?"

There were two people named Curtis Barry in the San Diego area. I took both numbers. The first wasn't home so I decided not to leave a message and instead call back later. The second call was answered.

"Hi, are you Curtis Barry?" I asked the man who'd picked up.

"Yes."

"Are you related to the Curtis Barry who lives in L.A.?"

"I have a nephew named after me. He might be in L.A."

"Was he interested in acting?"

"What is the about?"

"I'm sorry to have to tell you but Curtis Barry died yesterday. I mean, if it's the same Curtis Barry."

"My nephew wanted to be an actor."

"Okay. Can you give me his parents' number or any other family?"

"They wouldn't like that."

"But, they should know what happened to C.B."

"They know what happened to him. He chose a life of sin and depravity. Romans 6:23." He voice was so calm that it took a moment to fully register what he'd said to me.

I mumbled something like 'Sorry to have bothered you,' and hung up. I wasn't shocked exactly. I've always known there were people like that. In fact, most people were like that. But I lived in a gay neighborhood, I ran a gay business, most of my friends were gay. That was my world and it was easy to not think about the rest of it. It was easy to forget there were people like Curtis' uncle. Speaking to them, confronting them, only happened a few times a year and sometimes it overtook me in a surprising way.

And then I was angry, angry that I hadn't said anything, that I hadn't fought back. I imagined Uncle Curtis going on with his day smug in the knowledge that he'd condemned his nephew, that he'd condemned me. It seemed so mean. Could there really be a God who rewarded that meanness? A God who made me, and millions like me, and then wanted us to deny and reject what he'd made? I couldn't believe in a God like that and I didn't understand people who could.

Something occurred to me and I went out to the front. Mikey had just taken the chain from the front door. It was about two-foot-long, not unlike a bicycle chain. He'd insisted on it after the riots. I noticed that he was part way through doing the returns, which weren't a lot on a Tuesday morning. Monday was much worse.

"So Mikey, there's a tiny, very tiny, possibility the police might want to seize our computers."

"Why would they do that?"

"There are two detectives working on C.B.'s murder and one thinks I'm innocent and the other thinks I'm guilty."

"Well, you did wake up next to a dead body."

"Yes, but the blood—anyway, the important thing is that they may want to search the store and if they do they could take the computers."

"Oh my God, that would be a disaster. Why would they do that?"

"I don't know. Maybe they think I took notes in WordPerfect on how to kill someone."

"That would be kind of dumb."

I shrugged. Not as dumb as killing someone and going back to sleep—which apparently is what Detective Wellesley thinks I did.

"Anyway, we should probably have a backup plan."

The dress I'd sold to Wilma Wanderly had gotten me almost forty thousand dollars, which I'd put into a money market account and used to pay for my insurance. That was the something that occurred to me. Not that I had the money—I was pretty aware of that—but that I could use it for something other than insurance. Or rather, there was more than one kind of insurance. Making sure my business kept running was as important as making sure I kept running. They were kind of connected.

"So what would we need to do if the police came in and took everything?"

"Well, we'd need to buy at least one PC. Probably two. Would they take the printer?"

"Probably not."

"Why two PCs?"

"Well, this one under the counter is just a server. It holds our programming and our data."

"So they could just take the server?"

"Yes. But they'd probably take at least one other computer. Do you think they'd take all the backups?"

"Probably. They're going to take more than they need, just in case."

"Then we need to back up the backup since we'd have to re-install FoxPro, the system files and migrate the actual data."

"Can we do all of this without calling Wilson?"

"Probably. But I'm fine if we need to call...him. Really, I am. I'm fine."

Wilson had designed our system when we opened the store. At the time he was Mikey's boyfriend, but about six months later they went through a bad breakup. Bad enough that it had caused problems when we upgraded the system in '91.

"Okay, well, let's try not to involve him. So I need you to back everything up and then take the disks home with you."

"Sure, I can do that."

"Great," I said, and then went back to my office for a while. The conversation should have made me feel better, but it hadn't. In fact, it made me feel worse. I mean, the business would survive if Wellesley kept trying to make me guilty of murder.

The bigger questions was, *Would I?*

5

I spent the rest of the day at Pinx. Most of the time I was at the front counter out checking customers. Mikey was monopolizing the other computer making the backup. He needed a lot of three-and-a-half-inch disks, so he had to make a run out to the CompUSA in Burbank. He was finally finished around three, so I sent him home with a stack of disks. Everything we'd need in the event that our computers suddenly disappeared.

Carl and Denny came in a little before four. They were an older couple, basically retired, who insisted on working the same shifts. Missy called them Tweedledee and Tweedledum behind their backs, though they were good humored enough that I think they'd enjoy the labels.

"You live below Sunset, don't you?" Carl asked, when they came behind the counter. Below Sunset was the bad part of Silver Lake. Or at least it was if you lived in a little house with a peek-a-boo view of the reservoir.

"I do."

"Apparently, there was a murder down that way," Denny said. "We saw it on Channel 5."

"Did you hear about it?" Carl asked.

Why was everyone I knew so well informed? Reluctantly, I told them what happened. And I cringed when Denny said,

"Oh my God! Just like in *The Morning After* with Anne Bancroft."

"Sweetie, that was Shirley MacLaine."

It was neither, but I decided not to correct them. I took a major segue, then asked, "Do either of you know much about the Bible?"

Carl rolled his eyes at Denny. "What do you want to know, sweetie?"

"Are you familiar with Romans 6:23?"

"The wages of sin is death. Yes, of course I know that one. It's so cheerful, don't you think?"

"Carl, tell him the whole thing."

"The wages of sin is death; but the gift of God is eternal life."

"So, it really isn't as bad as it sounds?"

"We're all sinners. And we're all going to die."

"And we're *all* going to heaven," Denny added.

I seriously doubted that Curtis' uncle interpreted the verse in quite the same way Denny and Carl did. But it made me feel better to know that the way some people wanted the Bible interpreted wasn't the only way it could be read.

Tuesday evenings were not busy and the two of them would be fine on their own, so I was about to say goodbye when the bell over the door rang and someone entered the shop. I looked over and there was Javier.

Wearing a leather bomber jacket over a baby blue dress shirt and tailored gray slacks, he looked more casual than he usually did when working. I assumed that meant he was off duty. To make matters worse, the sun behind him turned him into a glowing silhouette. My heart started racing. I hoped it was a side effect from my meds—but it probably wasn't.

"Excuse me," I said to Carl and Denny.

Coming out from behind the counter, I walked over to Javier. We stepped over into the DRAMA section and I asked, "How are you?"

"I wanted to stop by and let you know we've released the scene—I mean, your apartment."

"Oh great. Thanks."

"You don't sound very happy."

"I am," I said. I was a terrible actor. I was a little bummed that he was so business-like, but I certainly couldn't tell him that —could I? "Um, do you think Wellesley is going to get a search warrant for the store?"

"She's still talking about it, but she hasn't done anything. I think she wants my support."

"She's not going to get that, is she?"

"No. She *is* trying to get a blood expert to contradict my opinion."

"Oh," I said, hoping that wasn't possible. Javier was right. I mean, I knew he was right since I was basically the sample.

"I've spent the day looking into your friend, trying to figure out who might have wanted to kill him."

"Any possibilities?"

He shook his head. "Not yet." He leaned in close. "He did have a lot of leather gear, clothes and whips and other things."

"Oh, yeah. That."

"So you enjoy that kind of..."

"No. I mean," I paused, wondering if I should tell him this. "I looked up his rental history and he rented some videos like that. But he never said anything to me. I guess he might have been waiting to see if we worked out..."

"So you're not really into that?"

"Not really," I said. I mean, I might go stand around The Gauntlet from time to time, but I wasn't about to join a motor-cycle club. "I mean, no."

"Good."

"Why is that good?"

"Um, Wellesley. You know how straight people are. They see anything even close to S&M and they think you're a serial killer."

"Oh, okay."

We stood there awkwardly for a moment. Then I said, "Um, I don't know if I should apologize or not. I mean, obviously there are things I never told you that might have made—"

"Yeah, um, no. I'm not really ready to talk about that."

"Oh."

I wasn't sure whether that was good or bad. I mean, it sounded like he was mad at me, but if he wasn't ready to talk about something that means he must understand, because I certainly hadn't been ready to talk to him—

"I should go," he said.

"Okay. Well, thanks for coming by." Though, honestly, I didn't know why he'd come. We could have had the same conversation on the telephone.

I took a step to my right, planning to turn back to the counter, not wanting to simply spin around like a top, and Javier must have thought I was moving to hug him or something because he jumped back. I froze and so did he. Wow. It was so obvious. He didn't want me to touch him.

I pointed and said, "I'm going over to the counter now. Have a great day."

"You too."

Except I wasn't going to have a great day. It was too late. I was already having a pretty crappy one.

When I got home, I found the door to my apartment unlocked and the window to my bedroom wide open. I walked in and just stared for a moment. It was a mess. A real mess. The drawers of my desk were open and most of the contents dumped on top, my armoire was also open, and all of my CDs and videotapes had been pulled out and stacked in front. My love seat—which was normally wrapped in a big piece of attractive cloth—was unwrapped and the dingy velour cushions flopped onto the floor. I closed the door behind me. That's when I noticed the dark gray dust on my hand.

Looking closer at my apartment I noticed that it was all over the place. On the door jambs, on my chairs, on the table, in the kitchen. Taking a deep breath I walked into my bedroom. The closets were open, my clothes on the floor. I walked around the bed, stepping on my blankets and clothes. I shut the window, getting even more fingerprint dust on my hands.

The bed. My God, the bed. Thankfully, they'd taken the sheets, but my mattress… I picked up the comforter at my feet. It seemed—oh, they'd cut a big chunk out of it. There were still stains but they'd taken the worst ones with them. I walked out to the kitchen and got a garbage bag and put the chopped up mess into the bag. I looked at my pillows. They'd taken the cases, still there was blood on one of them. I squished it into the bag. Then I shoved the other one in too.

Looking down at the floor, there were spots of blood on the wall-to-wall carpet between the bed and the window. I suppose I was lucky they didn't take part of the carpet with them. Still, it needed to be cleaned. I looked at my drapes but didn't find any spots. Well, that was something.

I did find blood spots on the wooden shelf that sat behind my bed. I'd either have to replace it or paint it. I'd had enough of the bedroom, I dragged the garbage bag out into the living room, and saw I had a message. Dropping the bag, I went over to my cordless phone—but before I hit the message button, I decided to re-wrap my sofa. I had to put at least one thing back the way it belonged.

When I was done, I hit the message button. I had one message: my friend Robert.

"Hel-lo dear. I have to apologize. It's been forever. I know. Entirely my fault. Call me so we can catch up."

I grabbed the phone and pressed speed dial and the number 2. That was Robert's number. Jeffer was number 3. I'd never gotten around to changing it. Marc and Louis weren't on speed dial, which I suppose was odd. They were now my closest friends. But of course, I almost never called them. I just went downstairs.

"Hel-lo!"

"Robert, it's me."

"Oh, there you are. It's taken forever for you to call me back. I called you yesterday. Yesterday!"

"You could have called me at work."

"The problem with that is that when you're at work I'm at work and I can't spend my time gossiping with you."

"You have gossip?"

"Oh my God, do I ever. I think Tina is shacking up with some guy." Tina was our mutual friend who lived in the same prewar courtyard building in West Hollywood. Robert's apartment was right next to hers.

"Who do you think it is?" I asked. Honestly, it was a relief to talk about something that didn't end in murder. Well, at least I hoped this wasn't going to end in murder.

"I don't know. I'm sure he's a screenwriter. She only ever meets screenwriters."

"Well that's nice—"

"Nice? It's terrible. There are only two kinds of screenwriters: successful screenwriters who date actresses and promising screenwriters who date D-girls until they become successful screenwriters and start dating actresses."

"Wait, aren't there also bad screenwriters?"

"Yes, but nobody dates them."

"Well, I hope she's happy no matter who it is. Listen, I want to ask you a favor. I need to buy a mattress tomorrow and I wonder if you can go with me in the morning."

"I'll have to ask Billy if I can come in late." Billy was Robert's boss-slash-boyfriend. "What a minute. You have to buy a mattress? Why do I feel like there's a story behind that? Is something going on with you? How's your health?"

"My health is fine. Nothing new to report on that front. I did wake up with a dead man the other morning."

"Are you serious?"

"Yes. Someone crawled through the window and stabbed him while I slept."

"And you let me go on and on about Tina's love life?"

"It was a nice break. It's all I've been talking about for two days—"

"Wait! It's just like that Jane Fonda movie, *The Morning After.*"

"You know, you're not the first to mention that."

"Not a bad movie. The costumes were terrible though. Of course, everything from eighty-three to eighty-eight is just hideous."

"Uh-huh. Anyway I need a new bed."

"You mean because he—oh, dear."

"FYI, people bleed more in real life than they do in the movies."

"I did not need to know that. And, yes, of course I'll go buy a mattress with you."

"And pillows, don't let me forget pillows."

"I wouldn't dream of it."

We set up a time and then said goodbye. After I put the phone back in its cradle, I went into the kitchen and found a bottle of 409 I had under the sink. With that in one hand and a roll of paper towels in the other, I started spraying and wiping every surface I could find.

Just before seven, Marc and Louis popped their heads in.

"I told you it was going to be a nightmare," Marc said to Louis.

"We're going to change our clothes and be right back," Louis said. "Have you eaten?"

I shook my head.

"There's leftover mashed potatoes. I'll bring some up when we come back."

Twenty minutes later they were back with a giant bottle of wine, the remains of the potato casserole, extra paper towels, a mop, and a bucket full of cleaning supplies. For the next two hours, we cleaned just about every inch of my apartment. Marc and Louis carried the mattress out to the garbage behind the building, barely managing not to kill each other since neither of them listened to the other's directions.

When we were finally done, Marc had a cigarette out on the balcony while Louis put the leftovers into my oven. I poured out three glasses of wine.

"We have Prodigy at the office," Louis was saying. "I went on the message boards and looked around to see if people were saying anything."

"What are message boards?" I asked. Like most computer stuff, this was a little over my head.

"They're kind of like personal ads."

"Except you can respond right there," Marc said through the open window.

"So, people are talking about C.B.'s murder?"

"Yes, but they're not saying much," Louis said.

"In other words, no one's confessed," Marc elaborated.

"I wasn't expecting to find a confession."

"Yes, you were."

"Don't pay any attention to him," Louis told me. "People are speculating that it's a serial killer. I think it's the crawling through the window thing."

"It's not though—right?" I said. "You don't think it's a serial killer, do you?"

"No, I don't. A serial killer wouldn't have tried to blame it on you. If the point were simply to kill for the enjoyment of killing, then they wouldn't have stopped."

"So you think the point was to kill C.B."

"Oh yes. Don't you?"

"Um, yeah. I think so."

Did I think so? Might it have been someone who hated me and wanted a murder pinned on me? No, no, if someone hated me that much they'd probably have killed me. Plus, I was pretty sure no one hated me that much. Except, probably, Cindy Peterson, Albert Wanderly and Consuelo Castellon. And they were all in prison.

"I'm sure," I said. "It was definitely someone who hated C.B."

"But no one comes to mind?" Marc asked, coming in and sitting down at my table in front of his wine.

"No. As far as I know everyone liked him."

"We're going to have to find out who didn't like him," Louis said.

Then our dinner was ready. We ate without saying a whole lot more. I think we were all getting tired. It was nearly ten.

After we tidied up, Marc and Louis left, promising to think about what we should do next.

I set up the cushions from my love seat on the floor, then put a sheet over them. I had only one blanket that hadn't been ruined, so I turned the wall furnace up and let it run until my living room was toasty. It didn't take long. I lay down, pulled the blanket up around my chin, and was almost ready to close my eyes when I decided to get up and put a chair in front of the front door, tucking it just under the doorknob. I did the same with the door to my bedroom.

I wished I'd brought Louis' Taser upstairs with me.

6

IKEA IN BURBANK WAS LIKE THE HOLY LAND; IT REQUIRED a pilgrimage several times a year. Of course, that morning it was an emergency pilgrimage. I had to buy a new mattress, pillows, blankets and sheets, and they had to be the cheapest ones in town.

Robert picked me up in his stop-sign red Trans Am with its T-bar roof. The car was supposed to be cool, but since it had several hundred thousand very obvious miles on it, it was anything but. Not to mention, Robert was too tall for the car and when he drove with the roof inserts in the trunk, which was most of the time, his head stuck out a few inches leaving his pink, sunburned forehead and fuzzy blond hair exposed. We careened down Hyperion on his shot shock absorbers, then got on the 5 going north to Burbank.

"I didn't tell you last night, but I think Billy is cheating on me," he said, his foot slamming on the gas until we were going almost fifty miles an hour—about twenty miles more than conditions would indicate.

"Why do you think that?"

"He hasn't given me a project in almost two weeks."

"What does work have to do with his cheating on you?"

"Oh gosh, I didn't mean he was cheating on me sexually... no, I think he's getting ready to hire a new assistant."

"Oh. Well, what happens to you?"

"I don't know. That's what I'm so freaked out about."

"I'm sure he's not replacing you."

"It's nice of you to say, but things at work haven't been, well, things just aren't the same."

"He wouldn't just hire someone else?"

"No? Really? How do you think I got the job?"

"Oh, I see."

In his place, I'd be worried about more than just the job. Something told me he wasn't Billy's first assistant-slash-boyfriend.

IKEA is a giant blue and yellow box. At one end was an outdoor escalator, which we and the other shoppers floated up like lemmings to the third floor, an entire floor of model rooms featuring everything they sold displayed irresistibly. As we walked in, Robert grabbed a shopping cart.

"We don't need a cart, I'm just buying a mattress. And some sheets. And a blanket. And pillows." Maybe we did—

"Please, I've been here with you before. Low-cost items just seem to cling to you as you walk by."

Unfortunately, he was right about that. We pushed through the automatic door and into the showroom area. On each side of us, living rooms, dining rooms, bedrooms. Small, neatly lettered signs told you how much each item was and where to find it on the first floor, the warehouse floor. It was like a zoo for home furnishings. Well, except that you wanted to move into the cages and live there forever.

In the center of the aisle were bins of smaller items. The ones that Robert thought would cling to me. And, indeed, they started to: washcloths (DAMMEN), two throw pillows in blue (CAPELLA) and a fifty pack of white candles (TORPED) to give to Marc and Louis.

"Are you sure the mattress can't be cleaned?" Robert asked.

"I wouldn't want it even if it could be. Besides, it's already in the garbage behind my building."

"Well, all right. You had a futon, right?"

"Yes."

"Do you want the same thing? Normally, I'd say you should get something that will help you sleep, but I'm wondering if you shouldn't get just the opposite."

"Ha-ha."

"Darling you slept through a murder. You may be sleeping too heavily."

"I'd taken a sleeping pill."

"That is so *Valley of the Dolls*."

Having known Robert for a very long time, I recognized that as a compliment. I thanked him and then stopped in front of a bedroom display. Immediately, I knew I was about to buy something I hadn't come for—well, something beside the things I'd already thrown into the cart that I hadn't come for.

In front of me was a black platform bed, headboard, book-case, and side tables all in one sleek unit. I needed to get rid of the brick and plank headboard I was using since it was covered in blood spatter. And this SKOT was the perfect way to do it.

"Oh my," Robert said, "Great Skot!"

"Oh shut up. I'm buying it."

"You realize you'll have to put it together."

"I'm not incapable of putting together a piece of furniture." And I'd probably ask Louis to help me. "Let's keep going."

I was ready to go downstairs to the second floor, where things were grouped by kind rather than displayed by room. That's where I would find the mattresses to choose from. If I could only find the stairs to go down. I said, "It's like this place was designed for rats."

"Rats with credit cards."

I noticed as we walked through that Robert kept picking things up and then putting them down. One of his curiosities was that he'd never really decorated his apartment—strange for a costumer who should care more about his surrounds.

Pointing at the pillows in the cart, I said, "You should go back and get a couple of these, they're cute."

"Oh no. I don't think so."

"Why not?"

"I'm not going to keep that sofa forever."

"Um, the pillows won't last forever. And they're really cheap." They were around five dollars.

"I don't want to collect a lot of things that I'll just have to throw away some day." He'd just described the pattern of most people's lives.

The way he'd said it, though, made me realize he wasn't leaving his creativity at work, like I'd thought for years, he was actually waiting for a boyfriend. He didn't want to decorate his apartment because he hoped to be leaving it soon. He'd been hoping that for at least five years. The idea made me kind of sad. But I did stop encouraging him to buy anything.

"You know, you haven't told me yet, who exactly was this dead guy you woke up next to?"

"Oh, um, I met him at Best Lives and we went out a little bit and then, you know, Valentine's Day."

"Does he have a name?"

"C.B."

"C.B.? Really? What's his real name?"

"Curtis Barry."

"Curtis Barry! Oh my God. I sort of know him."

"You do?"

"Yes, a few years back—oh God, three or four maybe—I was doing *A Chorus Line* in La Mirada. He was in it. I forget who he played. I do remember him looking damn good in a dance belt. Kudos for you. But then I heard he went into advertising and became this complete monster."

"I think he said something like that."

"There's nothing scarier than a reformed chorus boy."

"That's so weird that you know him."

"Not really. Do you have any idea how many people come through the costume shop in one year? Thousands. It's actually more unusual when I don't know someone."

But he'd met C.B. *before* he worked at the costume shop, so it actually was weird that he knew him. I decided not to mention that. Instead, I asked, "Did you ever hear anything suspicious about him? You know, anything that might have led—"

"—to his being killed in your bed? No. I mean, unless someone who worked with him in advertising wanted to kill him. But that was a long time ago too, wasn't it?"

It was.

I spent a fortune and I shouldn't have. The headboard was nearly two-fifty, the mattress (KALIF)—and I went with the best they had—was four hundred. Add on the light blue sheets (SOVA), the blue fake-batik duvet (NEOTTIA), and a cotton blanket (BALSA) and, well, the miscellaneous other things that had clung to me and the bill was a bit over eight hundred dollars. More than my rent.

Most of what I'd bought fit into the car, even the box for the bed frame when Robert folded down the backseats and used a bit of rope to tie down the hatch. To give us more space we put the T-bar pieces back into the roof and strapped the mattress on top.

Now I have to admit, driving from Burbank to Silver Lake with a mattress strapped to the roof of a Trans Am is not as much fun as it sounds. In fact, it's kind of a nightmare. The only way either of us knew to get back and forth to Burbank required freeways, so I had Robert's *Thomas Guide* open on my lap the whole way and my right arm out the window holding down the mattress. Robert was holding it down on his side.

Staying on surface streets, mostly San Fernando, Glendale, and Silver Lake, we drove at least ten miles an hour below the speed limit, getting flipped off twice. Really though, would people have preferred us to speed along until the plastic-wrapped mattress flew off our car and landed smack in the middle of their windshields?

In front of my apartment, Robert parked illegally across my carport. No one was home except me and Patty Wong. And since she worked at home I assumed we'd be fine. We carried the wiggly mattress up the red cement steps and up the stairs to my apartment. I have to admit, the way I felt about my apartment had changed since I realized how vulnerable I was.

No, no, I shouldn't think that way. The likelihood that someone would crawl through my window *again* to commit murder was actually very low. The fact that the first person to do so was still at large lowered my confidence in that particular idea, but I hoped it would eventually be true again. Right now, I had to face the fact that I wasn't going to feel especially safe until that person was caught.

I unlocked my door, and Robert and I went in with the mattress. Then we went downstairs to get the bed frame and empty his trunk. When we got to the street there was a giant brown sedan sitting there. An unmarked car. It was kind of silly that they were unmarked since they were always so obvious. Javier stood beside it.

"Oh my God, he's a cop, isn't he?" Robert said under his breath.

"Is this your car?" Javier asked.

"Um, shit," Robert said. "You're not going to give me a ticket are you?"

"No, I don't give tickets. I'm a detective. But you might want to consider parking legally."

"Oh, uh, yes sir," Robert said, though I think he was older than Javier. He untied the hatch, whispering to me. "Can you take this. I have to get out of here."

"But the bed—" The bed frame was heavy, I really couldn't do it alone. "He's not going to arrest you."

"You don't know that."

After dragging the very long box out of the back, he stood up and cheerfully said, "Okay. Gotta run." He ran around the Trans Am and jumped into the driver seat and then sped off.

"Your friend is acting kind of guilty. I hope there's nothing more serious in his car than a couple of joints."

"I don't think he does anything worse than that." Though, honestly, I had no idea what he might be carrying around for Billy Martinez. "You wouldn't mind lending a hand, would you?"

Javier and I each took a couple of bags and then tucked an arm around the bed frame. As we maneuvered up the stairs. I hoped he was there to tell me that they'd found out who killed C.B., but I doubted it. He would have said that right off—wouldn't he?

In my apartment, I led Javier into the bedroom, where we set the bed frame on the floor and threw everything else on the bare mattress. Then I turned around and walked right into him. I bounced off him and cleared my throat.

"You can—um, we don't need to stay in here."

"You want help putting the bed together?"

What? That didn't make sense. The last time I saw him he was disgusted by touching me. And now he was offering to put my bed together. He was totally confusing me.

"Oh, you don't have to do that."

"I know I don't. Let's do it anyway."

I gaped at him as he ripped open the box and began to take out the pieces. Once they were spread out, he tried to figure out how they went together. He was completely ignoring the instructions, which might have been a problem except they were pictures rather than words so they weren't very instructive.

"So," I said. "Why did you come by?"

"Oh, that's right. I wanted to let you know that we have found a single, unidentified fingerprint. Right hand, index finger. It was left on the outside of the window pane. It appeared the killer tried to wipe it off but missed."

"So you've got him."

"Not exactly," he replied, taking the last item from the box: a plastic bag filled with screws and plugs and other random pieces. "We did an AFIS check for California and didn't find a match. We can do a national search with the FBI, but there's a two to three month wait on that and the only fingerprints in the system are convicted felons. If this person was never convicted of a crime their prints wouldn't be in any system."

"Oh, I see."

"It *is* good news, though. If we come up with a suspect we'll be able to match the fingerprint against them."

"You mean, another suspect."

"Well, yes. We do know it's not your fingerprint."

"Whoopee."

"And, of course, Wellesley is saying it could be anyone's fingerprint who, you know, walked by and rested their hand on your window."

Actually, I had to admit she was right about that. Not that a lot of people were resting their hands on my window, but someone might have.

Javier found the little L-shaped metal tool that seemed to come with everything IKEA made and began to lay the bed out so we, well mostly he, could put it together. He continued talking. "We also got the autopsy results. Your friend was stabbed seven times. Four of the wounds would have been fatal."

"Does that tell us anything?"

"Yes, and no. It's overkill but not extreme. It suggests anger on the part of the killer, definitely."

"So you're ruling out a stranger?"

"Yes. For a lot of reasons. First, that kind of crime is usually sexual. We didn't find any evidence to support that. Of course, simply the act of stabbing can be sexual for some killers, but then you'd see extreme overkill."

"So you think the killer was angry at C.B."

"Yes, I think it's safe to say that. They also wanted to make sure he was dead. It's very likely he woke up and looked at his killer."

While Javier continued assembling the bed, I got the duvet cover out of its package and was unbuttoning the top so I could slip my new comforter inside.

Javier had more to say. "It appears the killer put his hand over the victim's mouth during the attack, as there was very little blood spatter in that area."

I didn't want to think too much about that, so I started to push the comforter into the duvet.

"We also found blood droplets along the balcony and down the stairs."

I stopped what I was doing. "So, Wellesley doesn't still think I did it, does she?"

"Now she thinks you had an accomplice. Maybe two."

"That's ridiculous. Does she really think I got someone to crawl through the window and just lay there while—" I stopped. That's probably exactly what she thought.

I'd gotten the comforter all the way into the duvet, shook it around so that it was flat and began buttoning it. Javier had the frame together and was working on building the drawers for the attached nightstands. I picked up the slats, which were attached to each other via canvas strips, and rolled them out on the frame.

As I did that, I managed to bump into him. I glanced up at him but quickly looked away.

"Uh, you know, I feel kind of stupid," he said.

"Why? I don't understand."

"I should have figured out what was going on with you. I mean, looking back it's kind of obvious. Your ex died of AIDS, right?"

"He did."

"And I knew there was something you didn't want to tell me."

"I guess I wasn't very subtle."

"You weren't."

"You shouldn't feel stupid, though. It's always easy to miss things we don't want to see."

He stared at me. I didn't have the slightest idea what he was thinking, but I was thinking about the way he stepped away from me at Pinx. I didn't want that happening again, so I got us back on safe ground. "What's going to happen to C.B.?"

"What do you mean?"

"His body. Did you find his family?"

"We reached his father. He told us to keep the body. Then his sister called later and said she'd make arrangements to have him cremated. Though it will be a little while before we release the body."

"It doesn't sound like there will be a funeral."

The drawers were finished and he'd slipped them into the nightstands. We unwrapped the mattress and put it onto the platform.

"It looks nice," he said. "Should we make it?"

"No, I can do that later."

He'd already spent too much time in my bedroom. I walked into the living room and then out to the balcony. Javier came behind me.

"Um, thanks for the information. It really helps to know what's going on."

"No problem."

He stood there, awkwardly, shuffling a bit back and forth. I waited for him to say goodbye, but he didn't.

"Well, I should get going," I said, though honestly I had almost nothing to do now that I'd replaced my bed and bedding.

Javier tried to smile and then walked away.

7

After Javier left, I made my bed and then put in a quick call to Pinx. It was Missy's shift and she promised me everything was fine. Normally I wouldn't trust her alone, but she said it wasn't even busy and that was probably true. Carl and Denny would be there soon anyway, so I lay down on top of my new bed and slept for nearly three hours. It was around six thirty when I was woken by knocking on my front door.

Groggy and with a bad case of bedhead, I answered. Marc and Louis stood there still in their work clothes, sans ties.

"Come on, get ready. We're going to Best Lives."

"We are?"

"Leon is meeting us there."

"I think the meeting tonight is about managing your healthcare," I said. "Do you really think—"

"Doesn't matter. We need to be there asking people about C.B."

They were, unfortunately, right.

"Gimme a minute," I said, before heading into the bathroom to struggle with my hair, brush my teeth, and put on a little bit of cologne. Taking a quick look in the mirror I noticed that I had a bad crease across my face. Thankfully, it would fade. Or at least, I hoped it would.

Ten minutes later, I was in the backseat of Marc's Infiniti and we were on our way to West Hollywood. For a change, Marc was driving his own car.

"I went with Robert to IKEA this morning. He actually knew C.B. back in his theater days."

"Did he have any ideas about why C.B. was murdered?"

"No. He did say he was kind of a monster when he worked at Imagination Station. But then, C.B. said that about himself."

"Do you think we should go talk to them?" Marc asked.

"I'm sure they don't want to talk to us. He's a former employee and all. They're not going to want to give out information."

"You're probably right. Of course, we could lie," he suggested.

"What kind of lie?"

"Well, most of what I do is merchandising, but I could ask them to bid a brochure. They're not as popular as they used to be; they'd probably kill for the chance to bid for a studio account."

"You won't get in trouble, will you?"

"No," Louis answered for him. "He's got his boss wrapped around his little finger."

"Oh, I do not. Don't exaggerate." Then to me he said, "She does really like me though."

"In that case, maybe we should," I said. It probably wouldn't lead to anything, but we wouldn't know for sure until we tried.

Then I caught them up on the forensics information Javier had shared with me.

"So when you say Wellesley thinks you had accomplices, plural, she means us, doesn't she?" Marc asked.

"I think so," I said. "Maybe you guys should get rid of those sleeping pills."

"She still can't get a warrant," Louis said. "There has to be more than just her suspicions. Now, if the blood drops went all the way to our front door, which I'm sure they don't, then she could get a warrant."

"No, Javier said the blood drops went down the front stairs."

"There you go."

I felt a little better but not much.

"I don't know, Louis. I think it's kind of exciting that we're suspects."

Louis looked at him and rolled his eyes.

West Hollywood Universal Church was located in a former storefront that shared a parking lot with The Pleasure Chest—which sold various adult toys and novelties. There was a cross on top of the building held there by a couple of wires. I wondered if it got knocked out of place every year when the Santa Ana winds blew.

Since I'd been going to meetings at the church, I'd found out that the building was once a men's clothing store. Most shops like that were now in malls. It was weird to think of one just right there on Santa Monica Boulevard, but I guess that's how things used to be.

Marc parked in the lot. Getting out of the car, Louis asked, "What kind of church is this?"

"Well—" Having never been to a service I wasn't actually sure.

"The name makes it sound like it's kind of one size fits all," guessed Marc.

"You know, I think they love everyone," I said, pretty sure I was right.

"All churches say that. Then they start with the exceptions."

Since we, meaning gays, were usually high on the exception list, I pointed out, "Yes, but we're here, so I don't think we're on that list."

"True."

Walking in, we were in a large lobby covered in gray industrial carpet. There were six or seven guys milling about, waiting for the meeting to start. One of them was Leon. He was talking to a good-looking Hispanic guy in his mid-twenties. When he saw us, he said something to the guy and then walked over.

"Who needs to go to the bars when you can come here?"

Before anyone else could say anything, I said, "Leon, please don't call my mother and tattle on me."

"Oh boy, here we go," Marc said.

"Tattle? Tattle?" Leon said, with mock shock. "Is there something I missed? You mean you *did* kill your friend?"

"Of course not."

"Well then, it's hardly tattling to call your mother up and tell her about something that was not your fault."

"I wasn't going to tell her. I don't want her worrying about me."

"But if your mother can't worry about you, who can?"

"Boys, we've come here to do something more important than snipe at each other," Louis said. "Although you were clearly in the wrong, Leon, and you know it."

"Whatever. The guy I was talking to is named Eduardo. He designs video boxes for a porno company in the valley, and he briefly dated your boyfriend."

"He wasn't my boyfriend. How many times do I have to—"

"He also thinks you killed him. I made it very clear you did not."

"Oh, well, thank you for that."

"Did you talk to anyone else?" Louis asked.

"Not yet."

"Did you get Eduardo's number?"

"I did."

Just then, Bartholomew came over. He was a well-preserved gentleman in his late forties. He wore an oversized jacket, black with thin white stripes, and a mustard-colored shirt. Far too trendy for his age.

"Noah, people are saying terrible things. Promise me they're not true."

"They're not. What people?"

"The police were here last night. My God, how many murders have you been involved in?"

I decided not to answer that. "It was a detective named Wellesley, right?"

"It was. How did you know that?"

"She sort of hates me."

"That's an understatement."

"These are my friends, Marc and Louis, and Leon."

Everyone said hello.

"So you were friends with C.B.?" Louis asked.

"Of course I was friends with C.B. He was a friendly guy," Bartholomew said. He didn't sound particularly sincere.

"I'm going to go get some coffee," Marc said, eyeing the table set up on the far side of the lobby. It held a large coffee pot and two trays of cookies.

As he walked away, Louis said, "No cookies."

"Spoil sport."

"So, Bart," Leon said.

"Oh no, no, no. Do not call me Bart. Do I look like a *Simpsons* character? Don't answer that. And no, I will not say 'eat my shorts' no matter how many times you ask."

"Okay. Bartholomew, you liked C.B., but do you know of anyone who didn't?" Leon said.

"Well, I don't think anyone really *dis*liked him. He owed Michael money so there was some bad blood there. He didn't seem to be trying to pay it back. And of course now— But that doesn't mean Michael didn't like him. He wouldn't have loaned him money if he didn't."

"Why do you think C.B. hadn't paid back the money?"

"He can't have been making much money. He had a small stipend from Best Lives and occasional freelance work. But I think the freelance was fading."

I glanced over to the coffee station. Marc was talking to someone named Skip, I think.

"You're just C.B.'s type you know," Bartholomew said. "Young."

"What? Me? No, I'm not that young."

"How old are you? Twenty-four, twenty-five?"

"Twenty-nine."

"Still. C.B. was in his mid-forties."

"Thirty-nine."

"Did he tell you that? Or did you get a look at his driver's license?"

Bartholomew seemed annoyed that C.B. liked younger guys, whether it was true or not. I wondered if he wanted to go out with C.B. They were actually closer in age that C.B. and I were. Maybe he was jealous.

Just then, Steve Meier, who used to help C.B. out, opened the doors to the church proper and said, "All right, you can all come in now."

We began to shuffle into the church. Twelve white chairs had been set up in a circle.

Louis fell in beside me. "Bartholomew seems a little touchy about C.B. We should put him on our list."

"We're making a list?" I asked.

"Of course. A mental list. And we'll be checking it twice."

"All right. I guess he's on it then."

Once we'd all taken a seat, the room was pretty full. There was only one empty chair. I felt a little awkward being there. This wasn't my regular group. I wasn't having trouble getting medical care and I didn't have much to offer. I couldn't even give people advice on how to get insurance. The only reason I had it was that I'd sold a valuable piece of Hollywood memorabilia, which was hardly a path I could recommend to others.

I usually came on Saturdays for the regular Men's Rap. Which didn't mean I hadn't seen most everyone before. People tended to stop by Best Lives more than once a week.

"Good evening," Steve said. "Thank you all for coming to the Wednesday night session on facilitating your medical care. I'm Steve. Most of you know me. I've volunteered to take over C.B.'s duties for the time being. Tonight, I thought we should put aside medical care and talk about C.B. Unless anyone has something urgent."

He left a brief pause in case anyone wanted to object and then continued, "I'm putting together a memorial for Friday evening at seven. It will be here at the church: coffee, baked goods, juice, nothing alcoholic—church rules. I'm going to say a few words, and I'm sure many of you would like to say something as well. Noah—"

I nearly jumped out of my seat when he said my name.

"Since you were with him—you should really consider saying a few words on Friday."

"Um, okay. I'll consider it." And try to figure out how to avoid it. *Maybe I won't go at all.*

"Wonderful. Tonight we should talk about what it means to lose someone like C.B. You don't have to talk about C.B. in particular, you can talk about what it means to lose anyone close to you. Certainly, we've lost many of our members here at Best Lives."

"It's different though," Dante said. He was somewhere in his thirties, thin and artsy. Had he said he was a photographer? I couldn't remember.

"How so?" Steve asked, modulating his voice in the way people do when they're consciously being kind.

"Well, he didn't die of AIDS. I mean, usually when someone at Best Lives dies it's like it could happen to you too, so even if you didn't know them it still hurts."

"Do we know why C.B. was killed?" Skip asked. Dark-haired with a bracelet tattoo.

"I'm not sure if anyone knows yet," Steve said. "Do they?"

Several people looked at me. I looked at my shoes.

"So, it could have been because he was positive," Dante said.

"No, I don't think so," I said, even though I'd planned not to speak. "I was right there. I'm positive and I wasn't killed."

"Maybe it was someone he infected."

"Let's try not to use that word," Steve said. "Infected has such negative—"

"Whatever," Dante replied.

"We should probably stick to talking about our feelings," Steve said. "We don't need to speculate on why C.B. died. That's a job for the police. Would anyone like to talk about how they feel?"

"Well, I feel horrible and I didn't even know him," Leon suddenly said. "I mean, the poor man was probably terrified he'd die of AIDS and then one morning he wakes up being stabbed to death. The irony is crushing."

I froze. I wanted to drop my jaw, roll my eyes and smack my hand against my forehead, but I couldn't do any of those things. So, I froze. Then I remembered Leon had come on his own. People may have seen me speak to him, but they didn't know I knew him.

"Who are you again? And why are you here?" I asked.

Leon shot me daggers.

"Now, now," Steve said. "Everyone has a right to be here, and a right to their feelings. And it's true that, as much as we all deal with shortened life spans, none of us expect to die suddenly, violently. I wouldn't go so far as to say it's ironic, but you—"

"Leon."

"Leon does have a point."

"We were dating," Skip blurted. "In November and part of December. It was intense. I mean, I thought... I thought we belonged together. I thought we still had a chance. I was hoping—"

And then he burst into tears. After that things took a turn for the worse. Michael and Eduardo had also dated C.B. and they overlapped, just like Skip overlapped with me. It wasn't dishonest exactly, C.B. hadn't committed to me or any of the guys he dated. Still, that didn't prevent people from being upset when they found out.

A couple of the guys said some dreadful and unfair things about C.B., and there was a moment when it seemed like the meeting was going to be more about trashing C.B. than remembering him. Then Steve interrupted, "All right, you're all entitled to your feelings, but let's try not to say angry things about poor C.B. Not everyone feels the way you do. There are more appropriate times to express—"

"God! I miss the seventies," Bartholomew said, interrupting him. "Sex was so much easier then. You meet a guy, you trick with him, and if you like it you do it again and maybe you do it twice or maybe you do it a thousand times, but there wasn't any of this dating talk. I mean the worst thing about AIDS is that it's turned the entire gay community into a bunch of teenage girls waiting to be invited to the prom."

Well, that caused an argument that lasted the rest of the hour. The two sides were: 'monogamy was the only logical response to HIV' and 'gay men were sluts and would always be sluts so we were all doomed.' Keeping up was exhausting.

Afterward, we stood out in the lobby for more coffee and cookies. Marc and Louis, who'd barely said a word through the whole meeting, were suddenly gadding about talking to everyone. I stood mostly alone by the coffee. Somehow I didn't make it into the club of guys who C.B. had dated and dumped. I guess because I didn't actually get dumped.

Leon walked over to me. "What was that?"

"Well, first of all, I couldn't believe you said that. And second, if anyone was going to try to knock you down for saying it, I figured it should be me so it didn't hurt too much."

He thought that over for a moment and then said, "Fine. Act like we're making up."

He leaned forward and gave me a strained hug. When he leaned back, I said, "Don't do that again."

"You do realize most of those people think you've already murdered at least one person?"

"They do not," I said, reflexively.

"They do. You have a reputation."

"Why am I not in prison then?"

"Technicalities. That's the main theory."

"Oh, my God. Well, who do they think I killed? I mean besides C.B.?"

"Your ex."

"They think I'm some kind of black widower who kills everyone he sleeps with?"

"Pretty much."

My stomach rolled. I'd been trying to eat a cookie, but suddenly it tasted like sand. I dropped it in a waste can as subtly as possible.

Marc and Louis came over and said, "Okay let's go."

"What on earth were the two of you doing?" Leon asked. "You were quiet as mice the whole meeting and then you run around talking to everyone."

"You'll see. Tomorrow night at dinner. Everyone's coming at seven; you two be there at six-thirty."

Leon rolled his eyes and said, "God, I hate it when the two of you plot."

8

THE NEXT DAY WAS THURSDAY, WHICH MEANT THAT MIKEY was at Pinx during the day and Carl and Denny were there in the evening. Basically, the day was covered. If I took a full day off, it was usually Thursday. When I woke up around nine, I decided to take myself out for breakfast and then run an errand or two before I stopped in at Pinx.

On Sunset, I parked and grabbed a newspaper before ordering the California Benedict at Millie's. Sipping my coffee, I read about the Oscar nominations that had come out the day before. We'd need to order extra copies of the nominated films that were already on VHS. We'd be bound to see an uptick in those rentals. Skimming the list, I didn't see too much that was already out. *My Cousin Vinny* somehow got a nomination, which was a surprise. I didn't even finish the movie.

The big movies wouldn't be on video for months. I hadn't seen *Howards End*, so I had no idea if it deserved its nine nominations; I did know it was inevitable that someone would add an apostrophe and make a gay porn, *Howard's End*. I'd need extra copies of that too.

I generally didn't go to the movies. It was a little too much like work. And besides, eventually, I bought everything. The only thing we had in the store that I was anxious to see was *Death Becomes Her*, which was up for one of the technical

Oscars. Marc and Louis had seen it at the Vista. They loved it and every so often would ask, "Do you remember where you parked the car?" and crack up. Though, not having seen the movie, I had no idea why that was funny.

When I was done, I drove north on Sunset to Franklin and then east down to the Shakespeare bridge. C.B. had lived in a deco building sitting right next to the bridge at the end of Franklin. I hadn't been inside, but I'd dropped him off once in front of the gray, two-and-a-half story building with garages in the back behind the lower apartment which was half basement. His apartment was on the first floor with a front door sitting at the end of a short sidewalk coming from the street.

I knew from our conversations it was an enormous three bedroom place that he shared with two other roommates: a woman who played violin with the Los Angeles Symphony Orchestra and a guy who did special effects for very low-budget movies.

By that point, I was getting really tired of explaining to people I'd slept through C.B.'s murder, so while I waited for the door to be answered I made up a story. One that I'd used before.

A thin, angular woman of about thirty-five opened the door and I said, "Hi. I'm from Pinx Video over on Hyperion—"

She looked defensive and blocked the door. "Yeah, I know it. My roommate was going out with the owner."

"Oh, yeah, that's Noah. My boss."

"What do you want?"

"This is awkward, but we think C.B. borrowed a couple of tapes and it would be good if I could get—"

"The police were here. They searched the place top to bottom. Do you think your boss killed C.B.?"

"Oh God no. He's like the opposite of a murderer." As soon as I said that I realized how dumb it was. The opposite of a murderer, who took life, would be someone who *gave* life. Which would be a mother and I was certainly never—

"The detective who was here, Brenda, she seemed pretty sure your boss killed him."

"Well, between you and me she's not a very good detective."

"Because she's a woman?" The way her chin went up in the air told me I was on shaky ground.

"No, because she's not—I mean, isn't that part of being equal? It's your opportunity to suck as much as everyone else—never mind. Do you think I could come in and look for the videos?"

"What are they called?"

"Um, *He's Gotta Have It* and *Malibu Pool Boys*." I wasn't sure if those were films he'd actually rented. Actually, I wasn't even sure they were films. They *sounded* like films. And if they were films I did know they weren't as kinky as some of the ones C.B. actually—

"I don't know," she said, frowning. "His sister wanted us to clean up his room and send her the valuable stuff. We might have already thrown those away."

"Okay, well, they are actually valuable." If they were real they would have cost nearly a hundred dollars each.

"Don't be stupid," she said, as though she understood the video business completely. "It's just porn."

"So, my boss didn't kill him. I'm sure of that. Did you know C.B. was going to spend the night with m—um, Noah?"

"He thought he might. He really liked Noah."

That might have gotten to me if I hadn't learned the night before that he really liked a lot of guys. And, who knows, maybe he really liked me more, but I would never be able to ask him. Okay, that part got to me.

I cleared my throat and asked, "But he might have been dating other guys. Do you know who they are?"

"What does that have to do with the videos you want?"

"Um, well, he might have loaned—"

She studied me for a long time. Then said, "There was one guy. It wasn't serious. They'd been seeing each other every month or so for a long time."

"Really?" This was different.

"Yeah, really. I'll call him and see if he's got the tapes."

"What's his name?"

"I don't really know it. C.B. just called him Daddy."

My mouth must have dropped open. Bartholomew had said C.B. liked younger guys, but he saw someone he called Daddy? What was that about?

"Um, you have a phone number for someone whose name you don't know?"

Her guard went back up.

"I think you'd better leave."

"But, the tapes—"

"I'm going to call Brenda and tell her you were here."

Then she slammed the door in my face.

Shit.

I went back to the street and got into my little red Sentra. At that particular point of Franklin the two lanes split, with the lane opposite me rising about ten feet above the other. They come back together just before the bridge.

Had that gone well? I wondered. I'd learned there someone named Daddy involved with C.B., but I doubted I'd be able to find him. His first name obviously wasn't Daddy and there were probably hundreds of guys in Silver Lake who were sometimes called Daddy. I was looking for a Daddy in a haystack.

As I got into the car, I noticed someone sitting in a small gray station wagon on the other side of the street. I couldn't see much more than the back of a guy's head and it barely registered. He was just a guy in a car, right?

Still wondering how to find Daddy, I drove across the bridge, following Franklin up into the hills. I knew it was a bad idea, it was easy to get lost in the hilly areas. I thought about turning around, but most of the driveways were either full or basically nonexistent with garages fronting right up to the street.

At the fork in the road I thought about sticking with Franklin, but it looked like it just continued up into the hills. I took the other street which was descending. That's about the time I noticed the gray wagon I'd seen across from C.B.'s was behind me. He must have made a quick U-turn to follow me—but why? Was it to follow me? Or was it just a coincidence?

I kept going, not very quickly since the street was narrow.

Looking into the rearview mirror I tried to get a look at the driver, but there was glare on his windshield which didn't help. Plus, he had the visor down, as though the sun was in his eyes— which it probably wasn't. It was after eleven and the sun was too high in the sky to be in his eyes. Not to mention there were a lot of trees blocking it.

He wore aviator sunglasses. And a hoodie. Which seemed familiar. Did I know him? Or did I just—oh wait, that bomber guy, the one they can't catch. That's why I recognized him. There was a famous sketch just like this. Unabomber, that's what he was called. Well, obviously I was not being followed by the Unabomber. Just someone with the same fashion sense.

I came to a stop sign. I could turn right onto Melbourne— the sign was right there, that's how I knew the name—or go forward on whatever street I was already on. The gray wagon was right behind me, just a few feet away. Part of me wanted to believe that he wasn't following me, that it was just a coincidence. Still, I hit the gas and jolted forward. I wanted to try and get far enough ahead that I could see his license—

He stayed with me, following closely. What was he doing? Was he going to try to run me off the road? Actually there wasn't even such a thing as off the road. The houses we were passing were only a few feet from the curb, and there were a lot of hedges and retaining walls to keep the hill from sliding away in the rain. So the best he could do was drive me into someone's bougainvillea.

I was driving faster, and now the road was again going up and up, so probably not a good idea. The higher we went the more likely there'd be a spot where he really could—

We came to another fork and I took the street that looked like it might go down to the flats. I really had no clue where I was or even the name of the street, all I knew was that it was winding its way down. The gray wagon stayed with me the whole time, even as we reached the bottom of the hills and were back in the flats.

And then I was able to take a right and speed down two blocks. Stop sign. A street sign saying Sunset Drive. I recognized that. It was an extension of Sunset Boulevard. Back at the Vista Theater, the boulevard veered south and the drive continued east. I had the feeling if I took that—I took a chance, a risky one, and pulled out in front of two oncoming cars. This would leave the gray wagon at the stop sign for a little bit. I had my gas pedal pressed all the way to the floor, my little car struggling to pick up speed. It was not built for chases, that was certain.

I stayed on Sunset Drive, hoping that it would feed into a bigger street that I knew. But suddenly it ended and quickly I decided to take a right, swerving without even looking, thrilled when I wasn't annihilated by oncoming traffic. Once again I had no idea where I was. The gray wagon was further back but still following me. There was no denying that now. I'd made enough wacky moves that it couldn't be a coincidence he was still back there.

Suddenly, I was at a stop sign. The street sign attached above the sign read Fountain Avenue. There was an automotive place directly across the wide street. I looked each way quickly and, completely ignoring what I saw, jolted out into the street—earning myself some screeching and an angry honk.

Breathing a sigh of relief, Fountain fed into Hyperion. My store was on Hyperion. All I had to do was get there before the gray wagon could come up alongside me and bump me into oncoming traffic. I kept my foot pressed on the gas. There were two lanes, so I moved over to the right. But that wasn't great because most of the slower traffic was in that lane. I popped back into the other lane a couple of times.

The gray wagon kept pace. It wasn't far to the store. A quarter mile, maybe a half. I sped through a yellow light just as it was turning. The gray wagon zipped through the red.

A truck pulled out in front of me and I nearly smashed into it. Slamming on the brakes I veered over into the left lane. The gray wagon was gaining on me in the right lane. Yeah, I was sure he wanted to push me over into the oncoming lane. I sped up, then zipped back into the right lane. It felt like it was taking forever to get to my store.

Looking into the rearview mirror, the gray wagon was

lagging behind me. I tried to read his license plate but realized it wasn't there. He didn't have a plate in the front like he was supposed to in California. Maybe he was from out of state? I kept going as fast I could, trying to keep a good distance between us.

Finally, we came up to my store and there was a metered spot out in front. I'd have to stop and parallel park. I could have gone a little further and down the ramp into the parking lot behind the store, but I definitely didn't want to be followed down there. I decided to chance it and came to a stop just after the space I was going to—

The gray wagon zipped around me and sped off. I tried to read his back plate, California, the first number was a 2 and then E? B? F maybe. There might have been mud spread on the license since I couldn't read it. Or I was too freaked out.

Since he was gone, I decided to use the parking lot in back since it wouldn't cost me all my quarters. As calmly as possible, I pulled forward and then drove down the ramp. Everything back there was calm, well, except for me. I was actually trembling. I got out, locked the car and walked over to the back door of Pinx.

I entered the store and before I could say anything, Mikey said, "You're shaking. Why are you shaking?"

I didn't want to tell him I'd just been followed there by a Unabomber look-alike, so I said, "I'm cold."

"Well, no wonder, you're wearing a jean jacket and it's not even sixty degrees out. Don't you have a winter coat?"

I did, but it was for trips to Michigan where 'not even sixty' in February was considered a heat wave worthy of shorts and flip-flops. "I'll warm up in a minute. How's business?"

"Slow so far. It'll pick up later. Your friend Marc called. Twice."

"Thanks. I'll call him."

"And your *Video Store Magazine* came."

The idea that it was 'my' magazine was a little subjective since Mikey always read it first. Also true of the *Hollywood Reporter*.

"And that guy is here to see you."

"What guy?"

"He's over in classics." Mikey lowered his voice. "I think he wants to look at the porn, but he's nervous."

We saw that a lot. Customers hovering until no one was looking. Silly, since they'd eventually have to hand us the video box.

"Did he ask for me by name or did he ask for the manager?" As I said it, I realized it was a dumb question. Mikey would have gladly told anyone he was the manager, even though he wasn't.

"By name." As I expected.

"Thanks. I walked back to classics to the bookish-looking man of about sixty standing there. He wore a rumpled wool suit with a contrasting vest and leather patches on the elbows. I didn't think he was one of our customers.

"I'm Noah, how can I help you?"

"Hello. I'm an old friend of Curtis Barry's. I wonder if I could speak privately with you?"

"Sure," I said, wondering what this was about. I led him to the other side of the store, out of Mikey's view, so that we were standing in between Romance and Suspense.

"How did you know C.B.?" I asked.

"He was a student of mine." I was about to ask where but he went on. "Do you mind if I ask, how old are you?"

"Twenty-nine. I know I look younger than that and C.B. was at least ten years older, so I guess you were expecting—"

"You're a clerk here?"

"No. I own the store. It's mine."

"Your parents divorced when you were still at home?"

"My father died, four years ago. Why would you ask—"

"And you still live with your mother?"

"What? No. She lives in Michigan. It would be a long commute. I don't understand why you're asking questions like this. I mean, if you're a friend of C.B.'s don't you want to ask about him?"

"Of course, I do. Yes. You don't have a lot of friends, do you?"

"What?"

"Depression? Alcoholism? Suicidal tendencies? Homosexuality?"

"You know that's really offensive, don't you? Yeah, I'm gay, but that's not a health issue, it's not a psychological condition —*who are you?*"

"Thank you so much. This has been very helpful."

"Wait a minute. You need to explain what this was about. Do you even know C.B.? You didn't tell me your name."

But he was walking out of the store. Over his shoulder he said, "Have nice day."

The front door shut behind him. I looked at Mikey and said, "I have no idea what that was about. Did he tell you his name?"

"No. He just asked if Noah Valentine was here and I said we were expecting you shortly."

"Thanks," I said, picking up my magazine and going back to my office. The morning was not going well. I put my hands flat on the desk to stop their shaking and took a few long, deep breaths. I was tired, very tired. Part of me wanted to go to Marc and Louis' kitchen, get my mother's sleeping pills out of the freezer, and take enough to sleep for about forty-eight hours. I couldn't though, so I dialed Marc at his office. A woman answered, "Marc Jennings' office."

"Um, is Marc there?"

"Who's calling please?"

"Noah."

She waited.

"Valentine."

"From?"

"Pinx Video."

"One moment please."

I was put on hold. Marc picked up, "Hello."

"You have an assistant?"

"Well, I have a third of an assistant. We share."

"She's nosey."

"Very. She's from the temp pool but wants to be permanent. Anyway, enough about her. *We* have an appointment at Imagination Station this afternoon at five."

"Oh wow, that was easy."

"I knew it would be."

"I'm having a terrible day."

"You are?"

"Yes, something weird just happened. This older guy came in and said he was a friend of C.B.'s and then asked me a whole bunch of questions—except they were about me."

"What kind of questions?"

"Were my parents divorced, did I live with my mother—"

"Did you kill small animals as a child?"

"What? Are you seriously asking me that?"

"No. Did he ask you that?"

"No."

"Didn't you read *Silence of the Lambs*?"

"I saw the movie." Mostly I remembered being scared witless.

"It sounds like he was profiling you."

"He thinks I'm a serial killer?"

"I have no idea. I think the police profile for all sorts of things."

"None of them good."

"Well, no."

"And then I was followed. I mean, before that I was followed. On my way to Pinx. I was sort of in a car chase."

"That's so Steve McQueen. Who was chasing you?"

"I don't know. He wore a hoodie and sunglasses. Like the Unabomber."

"Oh my. Did you call Javier?"

"No." Actually, it hadn't even occurred to me.

"I think you'd better. Can you get here safely?"

"Yeah, I'll figure it out."

"Meet me in the lobby about four-thirty. I'll drive from here. Hopefully, whoever's following you doesn't know my car."

"Okay."

"Call Javier."

"Okay."

"See you later."

He hung up.

Actually, I was on the fence about calling Javier. I really didn't want to. I should, of course, but I didn't want to. Not after the last time we saw each other.

I opened my desk drawer and took out his business card, which was silly since I'd memorized his number at Rampart Station. He probably wouldn't even be there. Which would be great. I'd leave a message. I dialed the number, waited for voicemail to pick up. But it didn't.

"Javier O'Shea."

"Oh, hi."

"Noah?"

"Yeah. I didn't really expect you to be there."

"I just got out of a meeting." That didn't sound like a good thing.

"Okay."

"What can I do for you?"

"Oh, this is silly but, I'm pretty sure I was followed this morning. I went to C.B.'s apartment to talk to his roommate—"

"You shouldn't have done that. It could be considered witness tampering."

"Okay, but it's not actually the important part of this conversation."

"It's not?"

"No. When I left I was followed."

"You're sure?"

"Yeah. I was followed from there to my store and I kind of got lost on the way so it really can't be a coincidence."

"What kind of car was it?"

"I don't know. I'm not that good with cars. I mean, I'm not terrible. I've just never seen one like this before."

"So, it's new?"

"Actually, no, I think it's older."

"Foreign or domestic?"

"I don't know."

"Coupe or sedan."

"Station wagon. I think."

"What color?"

"Kind of gray."

"Gray or silver?"

"There's a difference?"

"Yes."

It occurred to me I should probably learn more about cars if I was going to have homicidal maniacs chasing me. I should probably get a subscription to *Motor Trend*.

"Gray," I guessed. "I got part of the license plate number."

"Excellent. What is it?"

"It was hard to see it all. There was mud on it."

"That's a common trick. How much did you see?"

"2B. Or 2E. Maybe F."

"That's all?"

"Yeah. Sorry."

"Don't worry. Those are the first two numbers?"

"Um, yeah." I decided not to point out that one of those numbers was a letter. Or that I'm not even sure—

"Good. Licenses began with a two through most of the eighties. That means the car was either sold here new, or someone moved here and got the car licensed at that time. So it's probably an older car."

"Okay. There are a lot of gray station wagons from the eighties though, aren't there?"

"Yeah, there probably are. Keep an eye out for it. If you see it again, don't go near it, don't let them know you've seen them. Just try and get more of the plate."

"Okay."

I was about to tell him about the man who'd come to see me, but he said, "Stop talking to people. I'm not going to be able to help you if you keep behaving suspiciously."

"Um, I went to see my dead friend's roommate. Under the circumstances, that's not suspicious."

"You know what I mean," Javier said. The tone of his voice said more than the entire conversation. It said that he wanted to protect me, that he wanted to be a good cop, and that those two things didn't exactly go together.

"Fine. I'll take a vow of silence."

"Good."

To make my point I hung up on him without another word.

9

MARC WORKED IN A BUILDING ACROSS FROM THE STUDIO lot in Culver City. The building was eight or ten stories tall and looked something like an Aztec Temple. The whole way there I was obsessively checking my rearview mirror looking for the gray wagon. I had to park in the neighborhood next to the studio since I wasn't sure it would be okay to park at a meter and Marc hadn't gotten me a drive-on pass.

The building was faced in pink marble, each floor was successively smaller and in the center was an enormous glass-covered lobby. Looking up at the huge panes of glass held up by a network of metal bars that looked like monkey bars, I thought, *This is the last place I'd want to be in an earthquake.*

I went up to the security guard and said, "Marc Jennings is expecting me."

"Noah," Marc said from behind me.

"Oh, there he is," I told the guard then turned to Marc.

"This way," he said. As we walked toward a nearby bank of elevators, he asked, "So you got here all right. No one following you?"

"No. Or at least not in a gray station wagon."

We took the elevator down to the garage below. Getting off, we walked over to Marc's Infiniti tucked into one of the corners.

As we got close he pointed to the rainbow sticker on his bumper.

"We all went out for lunch last week to welcome our assistant. I drove. As we're walking up to my car she sees the rainbow sticker and says, 'Oh, you're a Christian. What church do you belong to?' I told her what it meant and she almost didn't get in the car. Now she's screening all my calls."

"She did seem a little inquisitive," I said, climbing into the passenger side.

"Yeah, I think she's making a list of everyone who calls me and sending it to Jerry Falwell."

Marc started the car and we left the garage.

"What did Javier say about your being followed?" he asked.

"That I should stop talking to people and leave this up to him."

"So I guess you didn't tell him we were going to Imagination Station?"

"No. I did not."

"Good."

North of the 10 freeway, right at the edge of West Los Angeles and Santa Monica, there is a warehouse district which looks nothing like the rest of the summery, oceanside community. This was an area taken over by art galleries, photo studios, small absurdist theaters and boutique advertising companies. There had once been a passenger train coming into the area, but that had disappeared decades before. The old station had not, and it had been repurposed as Imagination Station. I had no idea if this was its first attempt at being something other than a train station or not.

We parked in the small lot adjacent to the building and then climbed a short flight of stairs until we were at platform level. Inside, the station had been gutted and left mostly raw. The rafters above us were exposed, the walls were brick, the floor polished concrete. A heating and cooling system hung above us in large silver tubes that curled every so often into small vents.

The large, open room was filled with mod, metal desks, some of which were tucked up against portable pony walls. Half the desks appeared to be empty. A receptionist's desk greeted us, but there was no receptionist. Marc and I looked at each other and raised our eyebrows. This was not the happening place it once was. We wandered through the desks until we found a young man hard at work.

"We have a meeting with Julie Winters," Marc said.

"All the way back. You'll see."

We continued, and as we got closer to the other side of the station saw that the wall and windows that had once been ticketing remained and were now divided into two private offices. Julie Winter's office was the one on the left. The tasteful sign next to the door to us said so. Marc peeked in and said, "Hello. Julie?"

I followed him into the office where we met a very polished woman nearing forty. She was dressed with a bit more flair than most women showed in business, a navy-blue sheath dress with an orange silk scarf arranged around her neck and shoulders. Her thin wrists carried a collection of vintage, hard plastic bracelets.

"Marc, it's so nice to meet you. Thank you for coming. We're so excited about your project."

"This is my friend, Noah."

"Oh, well hello Noah. Please both of you sit. Can I get you water? Coffee? Soda?"

She stood up and stepped to one side. It seemed like she was getting ready to go get us something, but it was probably more to show us the four gold awards standing on her credenza. Even though I was a little thirsty, I declined since we were basically playing a trick on this poor woman.

Sitting back down, she said, "So, you mentioned a brochure when you called. How many pages?"

"I'm afraid I wasn't entirely truthful," Marc admitted.

"Oh," Julie said, her face setting like fast-drying cement. "How so?"

"We'd like to talk to you about Curtis Barry."

"Do you even work at the studio?"

"I do," Marc said. "I do merchandising for our syndicated shows. Hats, T-shirts, coffee cups."

"Do you have a brochure for everything you make?"

"We don't. I could pitch that. And of course I'll take a stack of your cards and pass them around."

Julie's face loosened a little. She opened a drawer and took out a stack of business cards, probably a hundred. She set them on the edge of her desk and waited for Marc to pick them up. He did, slipping them into his shirt pocket.

Satisfied, she said, "Why on earth do you want to talk about Curtis Barry? Has he applied—"

"He died," I said. "Murdered."

"I see. I hope you don't mind if I don't act sad. It's been a long week and I despise fake sentiment anyway."

An odd trait for someone in advertising, I thought.

"I guess that means you didn't like him," Marc said.

"I loathed him," she said. "As did almost everyone here."

"How long was he here?"

"Nearly three years."

"That must have been awful," I said.

"It was. Well, more at the end than the beginning. C.B. was like a shooting star. He shot across the sky, burned out and fell to earth. He had this natural affinity for advertising. He came in as a temp and very quickly he was saying things, having ideas, and everyone listened. His ideas were good. We hired him, promoted him, and within a year half the office reported directly to him. Then he began firing people. That was his way of solving problems. Fire someone. If a client didn't like our pitch, fire someone. If the printer screwed up, fire someone. He fired one guy for misfiling a single invoice. Toward the end of his tenure we realized he'd replaced his staff three times. There was no continuity so no one knew anything and they were all terrified of being fired."

"Why did you put up with it for so long?" Marc asked.

"He was good. The clients loved him. Money was rolling in and things were great—and then they weren't. He ran dry. Stopped having good ideas. Suddenly, it was as if he knew nothing about advertising because, well, he didn't really. He was trained as an actor. He understood drama, certainly. But persuasion? No."

"Was there anyone in particular who might really hate him for all of this? I mean, more than most."

"Oh God, he did fire a lot of people. You know, he didn't even learn their names. He'd just come in and say, 'oh, I fired the fat one yesterday.'"

"The thing that's weird is that everyone at Best Lives loved him," I said, trying to understand this.

"What is Best Lives?"

"Um, it's an organization for people with HIV and AIDS."

"Oh. He did tell me he had AIDS. I didn't believe him. Not that it would have made—wait, he died of AIDS? I thought you said he was murdered."

"He was murdered. Stabbed to death. Someone crawled through the window." I decided to leave out the fact that it was my window.

"Well, someone was foolish. They could have just waited."

My cheeks grew warm. "So no one comes to mind? No one who might have wanted to do him harm?"

"Well, I dealt with many of the people he fired, of course. There were phone calls, meeting, letters, even a couple of threatened lawsuits, but generally people calmed down and applied for unemployment benefits. I'd have to go back and look to see if anyone was angrier than what would be normal given the situation."

"You've kept that information?" Marc asked.

"Well, yes. When we fired C.B. he threatened to sue. So we pulled everything together in a file and waited to be served." She turned around and took a thick file out of her credenza. Dropping it on her desk she raised her eyebrows.

"You couldn't give us a copy of that—" Marc started.

"No, I'm afraid not. That would raise a number of legal issues. I will go through it and see if anyone stands out."

I glanced at Marc. There didn't seem to be anything else to

ask. He took out his wallet and pulled out a business card and handed it to her.

"Thank you," she said, then glanced at me.

"Oh," I said. "I don't have a card, but I can give you my info."

I pulled out my wallet, took out my Millie's receipt, and, accepting a pen from her, wrote down my phone numbers.

To Marc she said, "We really would love to bid some work for you. The people I have now are very, very good. They're mostly from Otis. You can't go wrong with an education like that."

"I'll talk you up," Marc said. And, I knew he would. That was just his way.

Since it was twenty of six by the time we got back to Culver City, Marc dropped me at my car and we both drove across the city to get home. There was a lot of traffic, even on surface streets, which was good because it made me very hard to follow. Still, I did obsessively check the rearview mirror.

While I was checking to see if I was being followed, I ran through all of the possible killers we'd discovered. If the motive was romantic, then there were at least six possibilities at Best Lives, not to mention the mysterious Daddy. That was a lot of suspects—and we'd just more than doubled them. If the motive was revenge, it could be anyone of the many, many people C.B. fired at Imagination Station. Were there more than that? It was a lot, but if there were others we might not even know to be looking at them.

Money was always a good motive. But C.B. didn't seem to have any. His borrowing money from, was it Michael? That suggested he was broke. And I didn't have any reason to believe he had a ton of money stashed somewhere. We went dutch on most of our dates. Actually, I'd paid a couple of times.

Once again, I had the feeling I hadn't known C.B. very well. That meant there could be lots of other possible killers out there that I wasn't even thinking about. Were we getting closer to C.B.'s killer or were we getting further away? I had no idea.

About that time, I pulled up to our building on the top of its small hill in Silver Lake. I hopped out of the car, opened the metal gate, and pulled it back so I could drive into the carport. Marc had beaten me there and his car sat quietly in his space. After I reclosed the gate, I went up the red steps to the courtyard.

Louis and Marc were setting the table for ten. Looking at the table I said, "So this is your surprise? Company?"

"Not company, suspects."

That's when I noticed there was a stack of six boxes, each containing six brand new glasses.

"That's a lot of wine glasses," I said.

"We're serving three different wines tonight," Louis explained. "Appetizer, salad, entrée. We'll be collecting the glasses after each course."

"And when I get the glasses to the kitchen they'll go into a plastic bag to be checked for fingerprints."

"So, who are the suspects?" I asked.

"Bartholomew, Michael, Dante, Eduardo and that guy Steve."

Most of whom had been romantically involved with C.B. or wanted to be. Louis and Marc were running ahead of me. If it were actually someone who was a romantic conquest, that is. I asked, "What if it turns out to be none of them?"

"Well, then we've eliminated them."

It seemed time consuming, but then it wasn't like we had to eliminate everyone in Los Angeles. Just everyone who might have had a motive to kills C.B. Of course, as I'd discovered on the way home, that was a very long list.

"Louis, I didn't have a chance to tell you. Noah's had quite the day. He was chased through the hills by the Unabomber and Hannibal Lecter came into his store."

"Really?"

"And then there's Daddy," I said. Adding to Marc, "I forgot to mention him."

"Back up," Louis said. "Tell me about the Unabomber and Hannibal Lecter."

So, with Marc's help I filled him in. When I was done, Louis said, "All right, now tell me about Daddy."

"Well, C.B.'s roommate said there was a guy he used to see every so often."

"A fuck buddy?" Louis suggested.

"Louis, no one uses that term anymore."

"An occasional lover?"

"And no one says lover either."

Before Louis could guess again, I said, "All the roommate knew about him was that C.B. called him Daddy."

"Well, that suggests some very interesting things."

"And not *all* of them sexual," Marc said. "It suggests that he's older than C.B."

"Or more dominant," Louis pointed out with a bit too much relish.

I cringed. I was afraid they were about to ask me what C.B. and I had done in bed and whether he was—

"He could also be bigger" Marc said. I relaxed a little. "Maybe he's a bear?"

"Where do you think C.B. would meet up with Daddy?" Louis asked.

"Well, his roommate seemed not to have met Daddy. C.B. only talked about him."

"So he went to Daddy's place or had him over when the roommate was at work."

"Ah, afternoon delight."

Marc gave Louis a look but ignored the outdated phrase. He said, "Well, it all sounds very clandestine."

"Maybe Daddy is married," Marc guessed.

"Which means Daddy's boyfriend could be the killer. Jealousy is an excellent motive," Louis said.

By the time I went upstairs to change it was ten of seven. I didn't have much time. As I hurried into the bathroom, I noticed there was a message on my machine. Probably my mother and I didn't have time for her.

I rushed through a quick shower, then put on a pair of celery-colored cords I liked a lot. They felt kind of warm and perfect for winter. I added a thermal undershirt, and over that wore a boxy shirt I'd gotten at SFO. I loved it; it was basically black with a white band running vertically on the front. The band was embroidered with martini glasses and colorful confetti. It was perfect for the dinner parties. On my feet I wore a wine-colored pair of Doc Martens. I tried to do something with my hair, but no matter what I did it landed in a pile right above my left eye. I pretended it was fine, promised myself I'd get a haircut soon, and went downstairs to help out.

10

CHET BAKER WAS PLAYING AS I WALKED DOWN THE STAIRS. Louis had brought out their boom box-on-steroids, which had a five CD carousel, two tape decks—perfect for creating mixtapes—and could play for hours and hours, setting just the right tone for the evening. Between the two of them they had a giant CD collection. They'd both joined Columbia House and gotten something like twelve free CDs each and the opportunity to buy one more every month for a year.

The table was set, but the courtyard was empty. I stuck my head into their apartment and called out, "Hello?"

"Come on in," Louis said.

He, Marc and Leon were crammed into the tiny kitchen. The rest of the wine glasses sat on the counter, Louis wiping them dry.

"What time is it?" he asked.

"It's ten after seven," Marc said. "Don't worry, no one in L.A. is ever on time."

"All right, quickly, these are the rules," Louis began. "After each course we need to pick up the glasses. Take your own glass and the glass of one guest—we're going to have to choose."

"Eduardo," Leon said, without hesitation. We all looked at him. "Yes, he's the cutest. Do you think I'm an idiot?"

"I'll take Bartholomew," Louis said.

"Michael," Marc said.

"That leaves me with Dante. And Steve."

"And Steve's date," Louis said.

"He's bringing a date?"

"Apparently." Louis went on, "So try to sit next to your person or persons, so it doesn't look weird that you're taking their glass. If it doesn't work out just adapt, okay? Keep an eye on each other and if you need to change whose glass you're taking that's fine."

"I have three people," I said.

"Oh all right, I'll take Dante," Leon said. "He's rather cute too. Look at me, I'm having a three-way."

"So, the four of us are just going to tromp in here with the glasses?" I asked. "Won't that look weird?"

"Not if you two help with the plates," Louis said. Normally, Marc and Louis did all the clearing. Suddenly, I felt guilty about sitting on my ass every Thursday for more than a year.

"Make sure to remember which glass is yours and which are the guests. Try to pick their glass up by the stem if you can."

"But don't be obvious," Marc added.

"Then when you get in here, we'll put the glasses into one of these Ziploc bags that I've already labeled. Two for each suspect."

"We only need one though don't we?"

"I think we should try for at least two," Louis said. "It's a wine glass that they'll be picking up over and over. It'll be very easy to smudge the prints or we might miss their index finger entirely."

"You've really thought this through," I said.

Louis just shrugged and continued, "We're having an appetizer course of chilled shrimp, cheeses and crudités. We'll serve that with a fumé blanc. Then we'll have a salad of field greens, sliced apples, walnuts with a raspberry vinaigrette. That we'll serve with a chardonnay. Then for the main course we're having London broil with brown gravy and blanched broccoli. That's paired with a full bodied cabernet sauvignon."

"This is all on *The Drinking Man's Diet*, isn't it?" I asked, barely masking my disappointment.

"Don't worry," Marc said. "I ran out to the La Brea Bakery at lunch and got two sourdough batards."

"Thank you," I said quietly. I felt a little weird about needing my carbs, but I was far too thin to be on *The Drinking Man's Diet*. And since I'd gotten my appetite back, Thursday nights had become my best chance to get a lot of calories.

"Can I have a glass of wine while we wait for people? Or is that against the rules?" Leon wanted to know.

"No, no, sorry, let's have wine," Louis said.

Louis opened a bottle of wine and poured it out into the glasses we normally used.

"How much of this wine did you buy?" I asked, realizing that one bottle poured four or five glasses.

"Three bottles of each."

"Yikes."

"Don't worry. It's from Trader Joe's so we didn't break the bank."

As we sipped the wine, Marc and I told them what happened at Imagination Station. Making Leon ask, "So, tonight is a waste of time? If it's someone who used to work at Imagination Station then it won't be anyone you've invited."

"Well, I don't know. I think it was good that you guys went to Imagination Station, but it's hard to imagine someone would kill C.B. over a job they lost two or three years ago," Louis said.

"It's not just a job though," I said. "Advertising is a career. I mean, what if C.B. fired someone just starting out and they never got another chance? That could cause a lot of resentment."

"It's a big leap from resentment to murderous rage."

"For someone who's balanced, but murder is not the act of a balanced person, is it?"

"I suppose that's true," Louis said, glancing at his watch. He frowned.

"What time is it?" I asked.

"It's seven twenty-five," Louis said.

"Oh dear," Marc said. "That is late, even for L.A."

"How was traffic?" I asked Leon.

"I took surface streets. But then I always do. Freeway phobia."

"That reminds me," Marc said. "If we can, we should find out what kind of car these guys drive."

"But is the murderer going to tell the truth about what kind of car he drives?" Louis asked.

"Good point," Marc admitted. "Noah, can you think of an excuse to go down to the street and look around?"

"I don't know. I mean, I only go down the stairs when I'm leaving."

"What are you guys talking about?" Leon demanded. "Why do we care what kinds of cars they have?"

"Oh that's right, you weren't here. Noah was followed by a guy in a little gray station wagon. He looked like the Unabomber."

"Why do you always save the best bits for last?"

"Hello!" someone called out from the courtyard. I was fairly certain it was Bartholomew.

Louis raised his eyebrows and said, "Showtime."

I rolled my eyes, pretty sure that was a line in about half the videos I rented. We walked out of the apartment, Louis carrying a glass and a bottle of the fumé blanc. Bartholomew stood in the center of the courtyard wearing a black leather coat cut like a suit jacket, jeans and a white turtleneck. On his hands, shockingly, a pair of gray gloves.

He must have seen me looking at his hands because he said, "I have a touch of neuropathy. Cold is the worst." He waved at the table. "I had the feeling we might be outside."

"I'm sorry," Louis said. "Maybe we should have eaten inside."

Not that there was room.

"Not to worry, I've got my gloves." He waved his hands at us.

"So, I want to get this straight, you all know each other?"

"We do," said Louis. "Noah lives upstairs."

"And I'm the wacky sidekick who pops in for every episode," Leon said.

"None of that was clear last night. But this is all so charming. I never come below Sunset, I was expecting a hovel."

"I hope you don't mind our subterfuge," Louis said. "We just wanted to go into Best Lives and ask a few questions about C.B."

"Because the police think I did it and I'd like them not to arrest me," I added.

"Ah, I see." He looked us over, considering. "So the four of you have some kind of murder club? Like a book club except with fewer books and more blood?"

"I don't know that I'd actually—"

"Exactly," Louis said, interrupting me.

"And you invited me to dinner so I could play too?"

"Right again," Louis said, holding out the glass of wine he'd filled for Bartholomew.

"Well, in that case: Steve Meier." To me he added, "I mean, did you notice the way he's just barreled into Best Lives and taken over? C.B.'s body is barely cold and Steve is angling for his job. Just like a straight man to think *he* should be the one in charge."

"Steve is straight?" Marc asked.

"Yes!" Bartholomew answered. "Can you believe it? Apparently, he got HIV from a blood transfusion. Hernia operation that didn't go well back before they were checking blood donations."

"Are there a lot of straight people at Best Lives?" Marc asked.

"No, there aren't. Three, I think. Maybe four. It's horrible too. You'd think they'd understand that they're in the minority and act accordingly, but if you correct them about even the tiniest thing they're screaming about discrimination and intolerance."

"You don't really think Steve killed C.B. to get his job, do you?" Leon asked.

Bartholomew shrugged. "Those boys in Beverly Hills killed their parents for money. Was that a good reason?"

Actually, as murder goes, it was. A part-time job with a small stipend, though—

"Hello?" That was Dante and Michael coming up the stairs. Both were dressed in khakis with plaid shirts and canvas jackets. They looked faintly embarrassed to be standing next to each other.

"Hello darlings," Bartholomew said. "We're here under false pretenses. They want to know who you think murdered C.B."

"Oh God, I don't know," Michael said. "I kind of thought you might have."

"Moi?" Bartholomew said.

Meanwhile, Dante hadn't said anything but was pointing at me.

"Well, you're both wrong," Bartholomew said. "I was just telling them I think it's Steve Meier. You have noticed the way he's just jumping in and taking over."

"He *is* very pushy," Dante said.

Louis handed them wine, holding the glasses by the stem.

"No thank you," Michael said, refusing the glass. "I don't drink."

"Oh," Louis said. "Can I get you some water?"

"No, I'm fine thank you."

"Michael, how many twelve-step programs are you in? AA, NA, SCA?"

He gave Bartholomew a cross look.

"Oh don't get angry. We're all friends here."

"I have an addictive personality," Michael said, though it was hard to imagine since he seemed so placid. Dante rested a hand on his shoulder, which made me wonder if they were seeing each other. And then I noticed that there were Band-Aids on most of his fingers.

"Why do you have all those Band-Aids?" I asked, abruptly.

"Oh, it's embarrassing, but I bite my fingernails. I'm trying to stop. If you see me trying to chew through the bandages give me a slap."

Well, so far this was a disaster. We hadn't been able to get any of them to even touch the glasses with their actual fingers. I glanced at Louis, he was obviously thinking the same thing.

Eduardo came up the stairs holding a bottle of wine in his hand. The only one of the guests so far to bring something. Very L.A. No one ever brought anything to parties. It made me hope he wasn't the killer.

Leon hurried over and took charge, leading him to the table and getting him a glass of wine. He wasn't wearing gloves or Band-Aids and he drank. Things were looking up.

"So, Michael, why did you think Noah killed C.B.?" Marc asked.

"Oh, well, since he started coming to Best Lives there have been rumors."

That was news. "About me being a killer?"

"About you being involved—"

"You weren't here," Bartholomew said. "They have a kind of murder club. I'm a temporary member. We're leaning toward Steve Meier being the killer."

"I wouldn't mind if it was Steve who killed C.B.," Michael said. "That way we can get rid of him."

"Do you have any evidence that it might be Steve?" I asked.

"No," Bartholomew said. "I wish we did."

"Well, you might want to stop accusing him since he's also coming to dinner," Louis suggested. "With a guest."

"Oh God! He's been seeing Erin Quigley. You know her, she's always there on Sundays for the spiritual hour." Bartholomew took a deep breath. "Let me see if I can get this right. She was a heroin addict, then a coke fiend, then a crack-head, and most recently a tweaker, geeker, cranker whatever the latest druggie fad is. She's like the history of drug addiction all rolled up into one skinny blonde."

"That's really unkind, Bartholomew," Michael said. "You shouldn't make fun of other people's problems."

Louis raised his eyebrows and, as if on cue, we turned to see Steve coming up the stairs with a tall, pretty woman nearing forty. She had long blonde hair and—though her clothes were contemporary—a hippy vibe. She wore a jean jacket over a gauzy dress and ballet shoes to keep from towering over Steve.

Everyone introduced themselves or said hello, whichever was appropriate, and then we set about getting everyone wine. Since it was my job to collect Steve and Erin's glasses, I delivered them. Holding the glasses by the stem I brought them out.

"Oh, you know something about wine," Steve said, pointing to my fingers. "You're carrying them by the stem so you don't warm the wine with your hand."

"Um, yes, exactly."

Steve carefully took his glass by the stem and held it that way. That wasn't good. We might not get a good print if he held his glass that way all night. While I was worried about that, Erin took her glass out of my hand and said, "Thank you." I wasn't especially worried about how she held her glass. I didn't think she was a suspect.

"Since we're all here, why don't we sit," Louis said, while Marc and Leon came out of the apartment with the shrimp, cheeses and veggies. We gathered around the table, which was really two tables: the round iron table that was always there and a square card table that came out when there were more guests. It was all covered with a purple, banquet-sized tablecloth that an old friend of theirs had "borrowed" from a caterer and never returned.

Once we'd all helped ourselves to appetizers and finished talking about what was what, Bartholomew said to the group, "So! Have you all seen Clinton's tax plan? Nothing but soak the rich, I mean is that fair?"

"Are you rich, Bartholomew?" Dante asked.

"Not at the moment, but I hope to be one day."

"One day had better come soon," Eduardo said under his breath to Leon.

"I heard that," Bartholomew said. "Just because I'm HIV positive doesn't mean I'm going to die soon."

"I meant that you're old," Eduardo said.

Bartholomew pursed his lips.

"So, really you're complaining in advance. Is that what you meant?" Louis said.

"I'm saying it's just not fair. Why should the rich pay so much more? What's wrong with a flat tax? Everyone pays ten percent and then we're done with it."

"But you can't," Steve said. "Ten percent to someone making say, twenty thousand a year is a lot of money while ten percent to someone making a hundred thousand isn't much at all."

"Nonsense, ten percent is ten percent."

"No, it's not. If you pay your ten percent and you have ninety thousand left over your quality of life is not compromised, whereas the difference two thousand dollars makes to someone earning twenty thousand is enormous."

Steve was making a good point, I thought, and Bartholomew a rather bad one. Bartholomew was now my chief suspect. He'd been very anxious to throw suspicion onto someone else. I also thought he was jealous of C.B., either because he paid Bartholomew no mind or because he had so many men interested him. And then there were those gloves. Neuropathy? Really?

Then we stumbled onto one of those odd conversational pauses that someone had done a study about and decided they came every twenty minutes. Michael ended it by saying, "I saw something interesting in the paper this morning. They've done a study in which they mixed three different AIDS drugs together and they did a really good job of killing HIV."

"Really?" Dante said, sipping his wine. His bandaged fingers gripping the glass. I had to wonder, *Did the killer know they'd found a print?* Could it really be a coincidence that so many of our guests had foiled our plot?

"I mean, it's still in the test tube phase," Michael explained about the article he'd read.

"Which means it won't be ready for ages."

"Is AZT one of the drugs? Because AZT kills," Eduardo insisted.

"Oh, God," Bartholomew said. "A radical."

"You know I'm right."

"When they came out with birth control pills in the early sixties, my aunt started taking them," Bartholomew said. "They nearly killed her. She had a blood clot in her lungs. It took forever to figure out why. It turned out they were prescribing too high a dose, like ten times what was needed. It's the same with AZT. They were just prescribing too much of it. If you have a good doctor—"

"Anything will kill you if you consume enough of it," Steve added. "Salt, sugar…"

Bartholomew glared at him—clearly unhappy to be interrupted—just as Erin asked, "Who is this playing? Do you know? Is this the radio?"

The stereo was playing a jazzy duet of "That Old Black Magic."

"This is Keely Smith and Louis Prima," Louis explained. "The stereo has a carousel."

"Oh, I want one of those," Erin said. "That was Elvis Costello just a minute ago."

"It was."

"Oh my God, I'd spend days on end deciding which CDs to play together," she exclaimed. "It would become my new obsession."

"Well, time for salad," Louis announced, and we sprang into action picking up the plates and hurrying off to the kitchen.

Louis put the plates he'd collected on top of the narrow dishwasher. "Grab fresh glasses," he said, indicating the glasses on the café table.

"This is a disaster," Marc said. "Bartholomew is wearing gloves!"

"And Dante has Band-Aids," Leon added.

"Steve keeps picking up his glass by the stem."

"Now, now, it's not that *bad*. We need to keep trying," Louis said. "If we only get Michael and Eduardo's prints, well, maybe it's one of them."

"It's not Eduardo," Leon said, emphatically. "He's too cute to be a killer."

"Just because you want to sleep with someone doesn't make them innocent," Marc said.

"Well, it at least increases the possibility," Leon said, though that was hardly logical.

"Do you think he knows?" I asked.

"Who?" Marc asked.

"The killer. Do you think he knows he left a print on my window?"

"He might have guessed," Louis said.

"Then it would have to be Bartholomew," I said. "He's the one who's covered *all* his fingers. You know, just in case."

"Can we get the gloves off him?" Marc asked.

"Maybe if he was closer to the heater," Louis said.

"Or we could spill something on them--" Marc said.

"Maybe. But right now we should get back out there."

11
―――――

"So—*STEVE*? WERE YOUR EARS BURNING?"

Steve looked at Bartholomew and blushed. "What? Why?"

"These boys have a little murder club and we were talking about who killed C.B. Your name came up."

"You don't really think—I mean, C.B. meant a lot to me."

Erin stopped eating her salad and placed a hand on Steve's shoulder. "What does that mean? Murder club?"

"They investigate murders. They've done it before."

"And you think I did it?" Steve asked, looking terribly hurt.

"We haven't come to any real conclusion yet," I said. "Just that, well, we know that I didn't do it."

"And that Detective Wellesley is determined to pin it on him," Louis added.

Things were a bit awkward after that point, since our guests were either afraid of being accused of murder or afraid they were sitting next to a murderer. And then, incredibly, things got even worse.

After we brought the salad dishes in, Erin—having figured out we were using fresh wine glasses for each course—brought four of the glasses into the kitchen to be helpful.

"Sweetheart, you don't have to do that," Louis said.

"Of course I do. Just because I'm a drug addict doesn't mean I was raised by wolves."

So that was four glasses that we had no idea who they'd belonged to—and certainly couldn't ask. So far, we had only successfully collected Michael and Eduardo's fingerprints. Erin put the glasses in the sink and said, "You boys keep working on the salad. I'll get the rest of the glasses."

"Oh no, you don't have to—" Louis started, but she was off, picking up four fresh glasses from the café table and then scurrying out of the kitchen. To me he said, "Stop her."

I grabbed some clean glasses and hurried out of the apartment. Erin was already at the table.

"Erin, please sit down, I'll get the glasses."

"Oh, well, all right."

I began picking up glasses, careful to try to remember which was which. I wasn't paying a lot of attention to what Erin was doing. I knew she was close, that she hadn't sat down like I asked, but I wasn't paying—and then she spun around holding a stack of plates with the tiny pitcher full of raspberry vinaigrette—

She crashed right into me. I dropped the glasses. Plates fell to the ground. The tiny pitcher spewed the remaining dressing all over the front of my shirt and also fell to the ground.

I think I yelped.

"I'm so sorry!" Erin said. "Your poor shirt."

Why did this woman have to be so helpful? She snatched a cloth napkin off the table and began swirling the raspberry stain around.

"It's okay, really," I said. All she was managing to do was press the cold dressing into my shirt so that it soaked all the way through to my bare skin. I think I shivered.

Marc and Louis hurried out of the apartment and everything seemed to come to a halt while we cleaned up. Well, they cleaned up. I stood there useless. Anything I did to help only seemed to make things worse.

Two of the glasses hadn't broken, but we had no idea who they belonged to. Having scooped up most of the broken glass onto a plate, they went back into the kitchen. I followed.

Louis said to Marc, "Okay, now it's officially a disaster."

"Forks," said Marc quietly. "We have to go for forks instead."

"Good idea," Louis agreed. "Except when you pick them up, try to avoid the flat part. That's where the best prints would be."

They left to go get forks while I stood by the sink dabbing my shirt. It was going to have to go to the cleaners if I was going to save it. I thought about going upstairs and getting another shirt, but I was afraid I'd just end up ruining it as well.

The CD player wound its way back to Chet Baker when things had calmed down enough for the entrée and the third bottle of wine. Louis announced it: "This is a Californian cabernet sauvignon." He'd opened two of the bottles already so we began pouring.

The conversation, which was beginning to get a little sloppy, turned to C.B., and the people Louis had invited as suspects began trying to figure out who had killed him. Without us.

"I'm sure it was someone he was sleeping with," Dante said, hurt inflecting his voice. "Present company excepted."

"You mean, like Skip?" Bartholomew wondered.

Louis tried to give Steve some red wine, but Steve put his hand over the glass. "Oh no, I have to drive home."

"Well yes, Skip," Dante said. "I mean, he was dating Skip at the same time as Noah. Or at least part of the time. Maybe Skip was angry that C.B. chose Noah?"

"I think that's very plausible," Bartholomew agreed.

The wine was all poured and we'd sat down again, about to start the main course when Patty Wong popped out of her apartment—as though she'd been waiting for the most inopportune time—and made a beeline for us.

"Oh my God, you're having dinner! It looks so delicious! I know you keep trying to invite me, but I'm just so, so busy."

Since we never invited her, Louis just smiled.

"Well, I just wanted to come out and mention that Detective Wellesley came by to see me this morning. She is *so* nice. We had such a pleasant conversation."

"About?" As Wellesley's chief suspect I thought I should ask.

"Oh, just this and that. Things I've heard and seen." The

way she said that made it seem like illicit things were happing around our building constantly.

"Don't worry, Lee. I said nice things about you. I would never give away any of your secrets."

His face hardened. "You don't know my secrets."

"Oh, but I do." She leaned in close and whispered into his ear.

His mouth dropped open. "Who are you?"

She smiled and said, "You know who I am. I'm Patty Wong. Well, gotta run. Enjoy your dinner."

The table was quiet for a long moment and then Louis said, "Dig in."

"Well, she seemed interesting," Bartholomew said.

"What did she say to you?" Eduardo asked Leon.

"Nothing."

"And—do people call you Lee?"

"No. Never."

Michael and Erin began to reminisce about their druggie days and Bartholomew chimed in with, "Remember when we thought cocaine wasn't addictive? Those were the days."

"Oh God yes," Erin said. "Guilt-free drugs and sex. What could be better?"

"You make it sound like you slept with everyone who asked," Steve said, tersely.

"Of course I did. I was in college and it was the Summer of Love. We all slept with one another." I started doing math in my head, which never mixes with wine, so I couldn't really figure out if I was right or wrong about how old she was. The Summer of Love was in the sixties, so—

"You shouldn't really brag about that."

She rolled her eyes. "But I never know if I like a man until I've slept with him."

"How do you decide if you like women?" Leon asked.

"Oh, I sleep with women too. It's such a refreshing change. Men can be so hard and sharp, while women are soft and comfortable."

Steve was now red-faced and looking down at his dinner.

The conversation had taken a turn that was not going to help us find C.B.'s killer, so I focused on my dinner. The London broil was tasty and the broccoli crisp.

"So, other than Skip, can you guys think of any other suspects?" Marc asked.

The guests looked at him blankly.

Bartholomew was the first to announce he was leaving, which sparked an exodus. So it didn't seem all that odd when we walked them down to the street level.

"You're so gallant to walk us out," Bartholomew said. "I have to tell you I was a bit worried about leaving my car on the street."

"Which one is it?" asked Louis.

"It's that little baby Beemer," he replied. "The silver convertible. I love the car, but the lease is killing me. It's highway robbery. Literally!"

Louis glanced at me and raised an eyebrow. I shook my head subtly. The baby Beemer was not the gray wagon that had followed me, so the likelihood that Bartholomew was the killer faded. Dante and Michael had come together, so as Bartholomew drifted off toward his baby Beemer we turned to them and said, "Which one's yours?"

"The purple Civic," Michael said.

No one had to look at me to confirm that it wasn't the car that had followed me.

Steve and Erin got into an aging Ford Bronco, with Steve at the wheel. It was red, so there was no way it was the car that followed me. That left only Eduardo, who was lingering near Leon and whispering to him every now and then. Then Leon came over and said, "I'm going to follow Eduardo home." As though that was somehow helpful to us. Then he added the more helpful, "He has a yellow Jeep, FYI."

"Have fun," Marc said.

"Oh, I will," Leon said, scurrying off.

For a moment, I wondered about what he was doing. Obviously, Eduardo was HIV positive, but I didn't think Leon was. He'd never said one way or the other. I tended to think he wasn't. Which made his sneaking off with Eduardo feel uncomfortable. He didn't seem to care. Sure, whatever they did would probably be safe, so it wasn't really a big deal that he didn't care. Except it was for Javier. And it kind of was for me. I mean, what if Leon fell in love with Eduardo? Though having known Leon for more than a year I would say he had no intention of falling in love.

Was that why it was different for Javier and me? If something were to happen between us would it be about love? And was that the problem? It was one thing to risk your health—a relatively small risk if you played safe—and another to risk your heart. Risking your heart was a much bigger risk; there was no way to risk it safely.

The remaining three of us climbed up the red steps. In the courtyard, we began cleaning the table. Louis went into the kitchen to get the bags he'd labeled and we put one fork from the entrée course into each bag. We had no idea if it would be enough.

"We should have put out water glasses," Marc said. We hadn't. Most people in Southern California didn't because of the almost constant drought.

"We'll have to go to Javier with what we have and just hope it's enough," Louis said.

They both looked at me. I tried not to grimace. Apparently, it was going to be my job to call him.

"All right, give me the bags."

"Aside from the fingerprint fail, what did you think of tonight?" Louis asked me.

"I don't know," I said. "At some point just about everyone was accused of killing C.B. I mean, except you guys. And Leon."

I carried the bags out to the courtyard and set them down at the bottom of the stairs so I could go back to help them clean up the table.

"What do you think Patty Wong said to Leon?" Marc asked.

"No idea," I said.

"I wonder if he knows her and just forgot?"

"Or if she knows him but he doesn't know her," I suggested. "Like in that French movie *The Return of Martin Guerre*?"

"Or the American version, *Sommersby*?" Marc added.

"So, you mean, like, she was in prison sharing a cell with someone who told her everything about Leon—except for what he liked to be called," Louis guessed.

"Yeah, exactly that."

Louis rolled his eyes. "I don't think she knows anything about him. She's like people who claim to be psychic. She just looks at someone and figures things out."

"Like that he hates being called Lee?" I asked.

"That's easy. If he wanted to shorten his name to Lee, that's what we'd call him. But we don't, which suggests he wouldn't like it."

That sounded reasonable. Patty could have heard us well before she met us.

"What about the gray wagon?" Louis said, as we walked into the apartment arms full of dishes.

"Just because no one drove it here tonight doesn't mean one of them doesn't own it," Marc said. "Lots of people have two cars or access to other cars. It could be someone's mother's car."

"Oh, right," Louis said. "'Hey Mom, I'm going to stalk this guy, can I borrow your car?'"

"Well, I doubt they'd ask that way, but yes, that's exactly what I'm saying. Any of our guests could have borrowed a car to follow Noah."

Louis sighed, "We don't seem to be making progress."

Once we'd gotten all of the dishes inside, I said, "We'll make progress tomorrow."

We said our goodnights and then I carried the fingerprint samples upstairs. Once I got into my apartment, I set them down on the dining table and immediately stripped off my shirt. It would definitely need to go to the cleaners. After I put on an old, gray CMU sweatshirt, the blinking light on the message machine again caught my attention. I hit the play button.

"Hi, Noah, it's Julie Winters, I was looking through C.B.'s file and there was one guy who took it really badly when he was fired. I mean worse than most. He threatened to sue at one point and I know he left some threatening messages. Why don't you call me back—

There was a noise in the background.

"Someone's here. I have to—"

And then she screamed. It sounded like the phone crashed to the floor. And then in the distance Julie was saying, "Oh my God! No, no, please—"

Immediately, I stepped out onto the balcony cum walkway outside my door and called down to Marc and Louis to come up. When they got there I played it again.

"Oh my God," Marc said. "I wonder if she's all right."

I picked up the phone and dialed. Javier wasn't there, but his voicemail picked up. "Hi, Javier, this is Noah. I got a phone call that I should talk to you about. Please call me when you get in tomorrow."

"When do you think she left this message?" Louis asked.

"Sometime after six," Marc said.

"It was here when I got home. I thought it was probably my mother. I thought I'd call her back tomorrow."

"We'd better go back to Imagination Station."

"Or we could call the Santa Monica police," I suggested.

"How long do you think it will take us to explain this, no less convince them? We'd better go," he insisted.

"I think he's right," Louis said. "It's after ten. Traffic will be light. We'll be there in half an hour. Maybe less."

"We've all been drinking though," I said.

"You'd better drive," Marc said.

"Me?"

"Yes, you drank the least of the three of us," Louis said.

"And even drunk you're super cautious," Marc added.

I gave up and we hurried out of my apartment and down to

the street. Marc stayed out and opened the gate while Louis and I jumped in.

"Take Western down to the 10. That should be the quickest," Louis said before I'd even started the car. I backed out of the carport, Marc closed the metal gate while Louis stepped out of my car and pulled back his seat so that Marc could jump into the cramped backseat. Louis got back in and I started off. After a couple of turns, I got on Melrose and took that to Western. Then drove south to the freeway.

We weren't saying much. I felt terrible. The possibility that we were responsible for Julie's getting hurt seemed very high. If only to make myself feel better, I tried to think of another explanation for what we'd heard.

"You know, maybe it's Julie's birthday and someone came to surprise her with a cake."

"That's an entirely different scream," Louis said. "This was definitely not an 'oh, goody cake' kind of scream. And she wouldn't have said no like that, even if she was on a diet."

"The hair on the back of my neck went up when you played it," Marc said.

"So it's because of us, isn't it? It's because we went to see her."

"Yes, whoever followed you earlier probably had a different car and followed us. We didn't notice. Besides, once you and I left the studio he probably knew exactly where we were going if he used to work there."

"You think he just waited outside for the staff to leave and then went in—"

"It seems that way.'

"There couldn't possibly be any other answer?" I asked hopefully.

Neither of them said anything. I got onto the 10 and just as Louis had said, traffic was light. I drove a bit faster than the speed limit and we got off in Santa Monica a scant fifteen minutes later. Marc remembered how to get to Imagination Station, so he directed me and then we were there, pulling up into the same parking lot we'd been in before. Except now it was empty.

"There's no car," I said.

"This is visitor parking. Her car may be around the other side."

We got out of the Sentra and hurried up the steps to the platform that went around the entire building. Hurrying over to the other side, I immediately saw that there was a bronze Mercedes sitting over there. Louis and Marc were already checking the doors. One of them opened and we hurried in.

"Julie?" Marc said. "Julie, are you here?"

We walked through the open area and went directly to her office, when we got to the door, we saw the light was on in there and Julie was on the floor in a small puddle of blood. Louis bent over and touched her.

"She's warm." He touched the inside of her wrist and then her neck. "She's got a pulse. She's alive."

Marc went around her desk, picked up the phone and dialed 911. As he gave them the information and told them that a woman had been hurt, I looked around the office trying to discern exactly what had happened.

"Julie? Julie can you hear me?" Louis asked.

She didn't react in any way. She'd been hit on the head. Someone had come into her office and hit her over the head, probably a couple of times. That seemed odd. Why hit her? Why not stab her? He did leave his knife at my place, but he could have gotten another. He might not have planned to— What did he hit her with?

"You know what this means, don't you?" Louis said.

"No, what?"

"It means everyone at dinner is innocent."

12

WE WERE WITH THE SANTA MONICA POLICE FOR ALMOST two hours. Fortunately, they didn't suspect us, particularly after we explained that Julie had called me in Silver Lake sometime between six and six-thirty. They could check that against the phone records. Plus I had two witnesses to my comings and goings with me, so that helped. We got home well after midnight and, after I locked the door and all the windows, I slept. Really slept. Probably for the first time in days.

I woke up around ten. Marc and Louis had already gone to work. They were planning to go to the March to Washington in April so they couldn't take any more days off. That was fine with me, I really needed to spend more time at Pinx anyway. And there really wasn't anything else to do. Once the Santa Monica police figured out who attacked Julie Winters they'd have found C.B.'s killer too.

After eating a couple of Pop Tarts, I took my meds, brushed my teeth, and put on the *Minty* hat Marc had given me. I figured I'd pop over to Pinx for a few hours and then come home, take a nap, and go in later for the evening shift. At that point I was so confused by the schedule changes I wasn't entirely sure who, if anyone, was going to be working.

On the way out the door, I grabbed my poor vinaigrette-soaked shirt. I pulled into the parking lot behind my store a little after eleven. Shirt in hand, I popped into the dry cleaners next door. Deluxe Cleaners was a typical dry cleaner with a small front counter and most of the space taken up by clothes hanging in plastic bags waiting to be picked up. There were some ironing boards in the back, but I got the impression they sent most of the clothes out to be cleaned.

It was a family-run business, Armenian I think. When I went in I mostly dealt with a dark-haired woman in her late fifties. She rarely spoke, which I attributed to her not speaking very much English. I would tell her what I wanted and she would mark my clothes with a bit of chalk. That morning, a dark, good-looking guy just a little younger than I was stood at the cash register.

"Hello."

"Hi. Um, I have a shirt I need cleaned. I spilled raspberry dressing on it." I didn't actually spill it myself but didn't need to explain that.

He took the shirt from me and was about to chalk the stain, when the woman I usually dealt with came over and snatched the shirt from him to look at the stain.

"Is blood?"

"No. No, it's raspberry dressing."

She gave me a puzzled look. Her son spoke to her in what I assumed was Armenian. They went back and forth for a minute or so. I would have had no idea what they were talking about except that all of a sudden I recognized two of the words the woman said, "Jane Fonda."

Me, they were talking about me. Apparently you didn't have to speak English to know that I'd woken up with a dead man next to me. The young guy smiled at me, a bit embarrassed.

"Please excuse my mother."

"I didn't really understand what she said." Though it must have been bad since he was apologizing.

"We'll have your shirt on Tuesday. The stain should come out, no problem."

"It is actually dressing."

"I believe you. My mother not so much." He smiled and asked, "Phone number?"

"What?"

"For the slip."

Sheepishly, I gave it to him. I felt ridiculous. I gave them my number every time I had something cleaned, so why had I acted like I had no idea what he meant? I mean, I guess he was cute and had a nice smile, and he wasn't a closeted police officer or, well, dead... He had a lot going for him... but I wasn't exactly ready. I'd been ready Sunday night, but Monday morning had really changed things.

He handed me a copy of the slip and I put it in my pocket. I said, "Thanks," and did my best not to run out of there.

Seconds later I walked into Pinx. I wasn't really that concerned about running a bit late since Mikey always arrived early and was so on top of things. But I'd completely forgotten he didn't work Fridays anymore and saw it was Missy who was behind the counter with the telephone tucked under her chin. She wore a black motorcycle jacket, a Nirvana T-shirt, a pleated Catholic schoolgirl skirt and Doc Marten boots. Her hair was dark brown, though in certain lights purple, curly and stiff with hair gel. When she saw me she waved as she continued her conversation. I turned around and went back to the office.

The first thing I did was check the schedule again. Carl and Denny were coming in that night, so everything should run smoothly. Maybe I'd stay until they got there and then go home to bed. Mikey would be working the day shift on Saturday and there was no one but me to work the night shift. Well, maybe Lainey would show up. Who knows.

For a minute I wished I'd stopped and bought some coffee, then I put my head down on the desk and took a little nap. I woke up at quarter to twelve. I decided to go out and give Missy a break and then zip out for some coffee when she came back.

When I got out to the counter, Detective Wellesley was leaning on it, smiling at Missy.

"We do have a petty cash box, but there's never more than, like, fifty dollars in there. And usually not even that."

"Do you have access to the books?"

"No, she does not," I said. "Missy you don't have to talk to her."

"Yes, I do. She's a police officer."

"You don't ever have to talk to the police if you don't want to and I'd appreciate it if you didn't talk to them about me or my business."

"All right. God, don't have a cow."

"What are you doing here?" I asked Wellesley.

"I hear you just coincidentally showed up at another crime scene."

"Imagination Station is where C.B. used to work. We went to see Julie Winters to ask if she thought any of her former employees might have wanted to hurt C.B. She showed us a thick file of people he'd fired and said she'd go through it. Later, she left me a message that she had someone in mind, but she was attacked before she could say who. Unfortunately, I didn't listen to the message until after ten. That's when we rushed over and found her."

"Yes, I spoke to the Santa Monica police this morning. They're not quite as convinced about this as you think."

"What does that mean?"

"What time did you leave Winters' office?"

"My friend Marc and I left around five-thirty, I think. We drove back to Culver City where I picked up my car, then we drove separately to Silver Lake. I got home around quarter after six, maybe six-twenty. Marc was already there."

"So you got home much later than he did?"

"I wouldn't say *much*. A little. I mean, I didn't ask what time he got home. He was just there."

"See, my problem here is that you could have driven back to Santa Monica, waited for everyone to leave and attacked Julie Winters."

"At what, a quarter after six? And then five minutes later I'm in Silver Lake? Do you not understand the idea of rush hour? Or physics?"

"Julie Walters was struck with a Clio three times—"

"A what?"

"A Clio. An award with a heavy base."

"Oh yeah, those were on the credenza behind her desk."

"As I was saying, it takes less than a minute to strike someone three times. You could have been out of there by, say, five after six and then been back at your apartment by six-forty, six forty-five."

"Except I was back at my apartment by six-twenty. We gave a dinner party. We had to get ready."

"A guy you were romantically involved with died on Sunday night and you're giving a dinner party on Thursday? You don't see that as suspicious?"

"I was at home with my friends either at the same time Julie was attacked or just afterward. It's not possible that I attacked her."

"What time did your guests arrive?"

"They began arriving around seven fifteen, seven twenty."

"So, either your friends are covering for you or you paid someone."

"Really? You think I paid someone to attack Julie Winters?"

"Sure, why not?"

"That's why you were asking Missy about money."

"Why don't you let me look around, that would speed things along?"

"No way. You'll need a warrant."

She scowled at me.

"And I think you'd better go now."

She straightened the jacket she wore but only managed to make it look more ill-fitting. "I'll be back."

After Wellesley walked out of the store, I turned and saw that Missy was standing there with giant eyes and a shocked look on her face. She'd heard the whole thing.

"Oh my God. She thinks you're a murderer."

"Yeah. I'm going to the Living Room for a coffee, do you want one?"

"Mocha Latte please. And a poppy seed muffin. Two, one for Lainey."

I looked around. "Is Lainey here?"

"She will be. Soon."

I sighed heavily and walked away.

"Noah."

I turned around. "What?"

"So, like, you're not really a murderer, right?"

I just shook my head.

By the time I got back from the Living Room with two sixteen-ounce coffee drinks and three gigantic muffins, Detective Wellesley was knee deep in the garbage dumpster that sat behind my store. I couldn't help but flinch. The dumpster and I had history.

Plus, it was disgusting. Pinx didn't add much to the garbage, nor did the dry cleaner. Taco Maria on the other hand put a whole lot of garbage into the dumpster, so Wellesley was standing in mounds of wilted lettuce and rotting pinto beans. To be honest, that didn't exactly bother me.

Inside, I dropped off the muffins and coffee with Missy. Lainey was there by then. She was a smaller, blonder version of Missy, except her T-shirt said HOLE. I hoped that was a band.

"You didn't get me a coffee?" she asked, clearly hurt.

"You weren't here."

"But you got me a muffin. How do I eat a muffin without coffee?"

I glared at Missy. After a beat, she got the message and said, "You can share my coffee."

As I walked way, I heard Missy whisper, "Don't cross him, there's a possibility he might be a murderer."

"God, don't even say that! My parents will make me quit again."

Shaking my head, I went back to my office. I sat down and tried to think of what to do next. Detective Wellesley had just derailed the Santa Monica investigation, so that meant I was now the primary suspect in two investigations. And that meant no one was looking for C.B.'s killer. Well, Javier probably was. I wondered if I should verify that. I mean, Wellesley might have convinced him too.

I was about to pick up the phone and call Javier when it rang. "Pinx Video," I said when I picked up.

"Pinx Video," Missy said, picking up the other extension.

"I've got it Missy," I said then waited for her to hang up. "What can I do—"

"Noah?" It was Marc. "I have bad news. Detective Wellesley was here when I got to work."

"She was here too."

"Oh, sorry. I would have called you earlier, but I had a meeting. They actually expect me to do things around here."

"It's okay. Warning me wouldn't have made it anymore pleasant." I thought back over the conversation. "What time did you tell her you got home?"

"I got home a couple minutes after six."

"And what time did you say I got there?"

"I think you got there at six-twenty-five. That's when you got home, right?"

"I think it was more like six-fifteen. But it doesn't matter. It's impossible that I drove back to Santa Monica, bashed Julie over the head and was in Silver Lake by six-twenty-five."

"Oh my God, no."

"But she's still convinced I did it."

"She probably thinks I'm lying."

"And Louis? And Leon?"

"She probably thinks they'd lie too."

That was bad. That meant I wasn't seen by anyone she'd believe until about twenty after seven when people started arriving for dinner. That was more than an hour. And that was enough time to go back to Santa Monica, bash a woman over the head, and then drive across town.

"I had to tell her everyone who was at dinner. I imagine she'll be trying to talk to them all."

"Oh God."

"What does Javier say?" Marc asked.

"I was just about to call him."

"I called over to Imagination Station," he said.

"You did?"

"I wanted to see if there was anyone there who could get us the file that Julie showed us. No one answered."

"It's probably still a crime scene," I said. Recent experience had told me the police stayed for quite a while.

"Yeah, that's what I thought. I'll try again this afternoon."

Someone said something to Marc that I couldn't understand. Then he said, "I'm on a call." Into the phone he said, "I swear she's watching me. How do I tell her I don't want an assistant? Ugh, I've got to go."

He hung up on me, which was just as well. I was hardly the person to give advice on employees. Two of mine at that very moment were inappropriately dressed and eating at the front counter. I walked up to Missy and Lainey as they were chattering away while finishing up their muffins. I looked around the store and saw there were a couple of people browsing.

On the back counter there was a tall stack of tapes in their black and brown boxes. "Can we get those tapes checked in?"

Missy frowned at me and moved the tapes from the back counter to the front. Then she opened the top one and typed the title into the computer.

"Noah, I know I'm on the schedule tomorrow night," Lainey said.

Here it comes, I thought. The dead grandmother.

"But my aunt died and I have to go to the memorial."

"I'm glad I'm not a member of your family," I said.

"What does that mean?"

"It means the mortality rate is really high."

Lainey's face paled and her eyes filled with tears. "Excuse me," she said as she ran out from behind the counter. I looked at Missy.

"Nice."

"So, you mean her aunt really did die?"

"Uh-huh."

"Well how was I to know. I mean, she lost three grand-mothers in two—wait, that wasn't real, was it?"

"No, her grandmothers are fine. I mean, one of them is really upset right now."

"Oh God. Just get the videos checked in, okay?"

"Yes, boss."

I went back to my office and decided I'd poke around until around one o'clock when it would be time to give Lainey and Missy a break to go have lunch. They could take turns, but I knew that would just get them complaining, and there was really no reason not to let them go together since I was there. What was really on my mind was whether or not Detective Wellesley was still out back going through the dumpster.

The phone rang. I decided to let Missy do her job and answer it, so it rang about six times. I was about to give up and answer myself when it stopped ringing. A moment later the intercom buzzed. I picked up.

"It's for you," Missy said.

"Who is it?"

"I dunno," said, hanging up on me.

I pressed the blinking button to pick up the call. "Hello?"

It was Javier. He didn't bother with hello, instead just asking, "Have you seen Wellesley?"

"She's in the dumpster behind my building."

"Oh shit."

"Close, smelly garbage."

"Very funny. That isn't good, though."

"She looked like she was enjoying herself," I said, though in all honesty she'd given me her standard scowl when I walked by.

"What happened in Santa Monica?"

Briefly I recounted what we'd done the evening before—well, I did leave out our lame attempt to collect fingerprints—and that morning's conversation with Wellesley.

"You do remember I told you to stop talking to people."

"Well, yes, I do remember that." Which is why I didn't mention the dinner party.

"And you see that you're now connected to a second crime?"

"In all fairness, I have to point out that it is *very* unusual for people to get attacked just because I talked to them."

As soon as I said that I had to wonder if it could actually be true. It had been a rather busy year.

"Look," I continued. "All that needs to happen now is somebody needs to find Julie's file and look through it. The person who killed C.B. and attacked Julie Winters is in there."

"Yeah, the Santa Monica Police said you talked about a file. It's not there."

"What?"

"There's no file."

"The killer must have taken it."

"Probably. Santa Monica is talking to her employees to see if there's another way to access the information."

"So they don't think it's me?"

"Not really, no. I've talked to them. They're not quite as interested in you as Wellesley would like them to be."

"You mean she was lying to me?"

"Yes, well, we do it all the time. It's how we put pressure on suspects."

"Oh, so I was just supposed to confess."

"She would have liked that, yes."

"Is she going to be able to get a search warrant to search my apartment and my business?"

"Only if she finds something out there in the garbage."

"Great," I said, fairly certain there wasn't anything incriminating she could find in that dumpster. I mean, day-old lettuce wasn't evidence of anything, right?

"I owe you an apology," he said.

"For what?"

"A guy came by your video store. He asked you a bunch of questions."

"How did you—did you have something to do with that?"

"No. It was Wellesley. I should have warned you."

"Who was he?"

"Dr. Sidney Folsom. He's written a very influential paper on hero syndrome."

"What is that?"

"Hero syndrome is a condition where a person commits a crime or puts someone in danger so they can save them. It happens with fire fighters sometimes. They start fires in order to be a hero by putting them out."

"That doesn't have anything to do with—wait, are you saying that Wellesley thinks I killed C.B. so I could solve his murder?"

"That's the theory."

"But—if I killed him then I'm definitely not a hero."

"I think the idea is that you'll find someone else to blame it on."

"That's crazy." I was about to say I couldn't pin a murder on an innocent person, but that's what Wellesley was trying to do to me so maybe it wasn't that far-fetched. "But I didn't fit. I mean, I answered most of his questions with a no. So I don't fit his profile."

"Yes, he says you're atypical, but he's still convinced you killed C.B. for the attention. He wants to study you. After you're put in prison, of course."

That was creepy. And very scary.

"Look, I have to go," Javier said.

"One second."

"What?"

I bit my lip. I didn't want to say this but I had to. "Last night, before we went to Santa Monica, we had a bunch of guys from Best Lives over and we collected their fingerprints on glasses and silverware. And they're in plastic bags. Labeled."

There was a long pause. "That's actually kind of smart."

"It was Louis' idea. When can you come by and get them?"

"I don't know. I'll have to call you. Okay, that was smart but wrong. Do you understand me?"

I nodded my head, which was pointless since we were on the phone. "Yes, yes, I understand."

"Now do me a favor—no that's not what I mean—Do yourself a favor and don't do anything else. Smart, dumb, doesn't matter. Just go about your business as though nothing has happened. Leave this to me."

"Of course," I said, because I always did.

"No, I want you to actually mean it."

"I do, I do mean it."

And I did mean it. All afternoon.

13

I STAYED AT PINX UNTIL NEARLY SIX. THINGS ALWAYS BEGAN to pick up around four-thirty on Fridays and were at their peak by six-thirty or seven. I really should have stayed longer, but C.B.'s memorial was at seven and I still had to go home, change, meet up with Marc and Louis, and drive to West Hollywood.

After a quick shower, I was staring at my closet wondering what I should wear. Since a memorial and a funeral were basically the same thing, black seemed to be in order. I had a suit from Jeffer's funeral, but it was already almost three years old and was a bit too *Miami Vice*. My only excuse for that was that I was grieving when I bought it.

I also had a black jacket with shoulder pads and a chalk window pane pattern that I'd loved at first but now made me feel a bit too much like a pimp. Unfortunately, those were my two primary choices if I wanted to be formal. So I decided to go with informal and put on my black 501s, a black turtleneck, my Docs, and a jean jacket. Wearing mostly black was respectful, right?

I went downstairs and found that Marc and Louis were not quite ready. Well, Louis was ready, dressed in a somber brown suit; Marc was still getting dressed.

"I'm glad you're here," Louis said. "I want you to take this and keep it with you."

He picked the Taser up off the coffee table and held it out to me.

"Oh, I don't think I need that."

"After that woman was attacked last night, I think you need to start carrying it. Everywhere."

"But, I can't—"

"You're going to have to."

I sighed. I really didn't need a Taser—did I? I mean, I might be able to leave the window open again if I slept with the Taser under my pillow. And it had been a little stuffy the night before.

"All right. Thanks," I said, shoving it into the left breast pocket of my jean jacket."

"How was your day?" he asked.

"Busy. Wellesley stopped by to tell me she still thinks I killed C.B."

"Then who attacked Julie Winters?"

"Me. In an attempt to divert suspicion."

"What does Javier say?"

"That if I minded my own business I wouldn't be in this mess."

"I don't know. Wellesley thinks you murdered someone. That kind of is your business."

Marc came out of the bedroom wearing a charcoal gray suit with a light gray shirt and a black tie. He looked a little like a black-and-white photo with his face colorized.

"Sorry, sorry, sorry. How late are we?"

"Relax," Louis said. "Nothing in L.A. starts on time."

Glancing at his watch, Marc said, "You need to drive fast. I don't think we'll get there until ten after."

"We'll be fine."

We left the apartment and walked down the steps to the street. As Louis pulled Marc's Infiniti of the carport, Marc and I stood at the curb waiting.

"I called over to St. John's hospital," he said. "I found out that Julie is still unconscious, possibly in a coma."

"What's the difference?"

"I'm not sure. I think you have to be unconscious for a while before they call it a coma."

"So you called and they just gave you that information?"

"Well, no. I had to pretend to be Julie's cousin from Tennessee." He continued in a Southern accent, "We all just have to know how our poor, poor Julie is feeling. Lordy, she just has to get better. Though we know y'all are doin' everything you can for our poor, poor girl."

I thought he was laying it on a bit thick. I asked, "And they bought that?"

"Hook, line and sinker," he said, climbing into the passenger side of the Infiniti. I climbed into the back.

"Did they have any idea when she might wake up?"

Pinching his voice to imitate the nurse he'd talked to. "Head injuries are notoriously hard to predict."

Louis, who'd clearly heard this before, rolled his eyes in the rear view mirror at me. He turned on the radio, which was tuned to NPR. The news was talking about Bosnian Peace talks being rejected, and I have to be honest and admit that I don't know where Bosnia is. Or for that matter who it was they were supposed to be talking peace with. I'm sure the conflict had something to do with religion or money or both. Since I'd never been especially good at either I zoned out.

As we parked in the lot between the church and The Pleasure Chest, I realized I'd never actually been to West Hollywood Universal Church when it was used as a church. As we walked into the empty lobby, I realized we were late. They'd already started. Apparently on time.

We slipped into some seats at the back of the church. I noticed immediately that Javier and Detective Wellesley were standing on the other side of the room. That was pretty common police procedure, coming to the funeral of the victim. I'd seen it on some TV show. *Columbo*, maybe, when I was a kid. My mother and I would watch it. But then, I think it came back... anyway, the police were there in the back of the church. Which made me wonder, was C.B.'s killer actually somewhere in the room? I doubted it. I knew a lot of these people, by sight at least. And the event hadn't been publicized. How would the killer even know about this?

I did my best to ignore Wellesley because she scared me, and Javier because he also scared me but for very different reasons. Turning my attention to the reverend, I realized I'd never actually seen her before. Or rather, I'd never seen her and known it was her. She was there the very first time I'd come to Best Lives, the day I met C.B. She was sitting in the first office—which is hers—and had told me he was running late. I'd assumed she was some kind of secretary, and now I always had the feeling I should apologize for the error.

Everyone called her Reverend Emily. The first time I'd seen her I'd thought she was in her early twenties, but looking at her now I revised that to nearing thirty. She was a small woman, with light brown hair cut into an overgrown pixie. That night she wore a red satin clerical robe with a long sash around her neck that was decorated with a rainbow flag and many different religious symbols. She was saying:

"Most religions seek answers, but we Universalists seek questions, for it is only when asking the right questions that you receive the right answers. People often ask me if God exists. That's the wrong question. Because whether God exists or not is something we cannot know in this life. It's a question only answered in death. Better to ask, if God exists what is He? What does He want from us? And does He want anything from us?"

I was already beginning to drift off. It was a Pavlovian response; whenever my mother took me to church as a child I'd be asleep seconds after sitting down. And now it was happening again. Reverend Emily was continuing and my eyes were falling shut.

"Imagine what an all-powerful Supreme Being would be like; a being that has always existed and will always exist. Would that being view sin and evil in the way we view it? Or could these things have an entirely different meaning? You see, when people ask, 'Why does God permit evil?' The answer is that it is not evil to God. Things that we find horrific, genocides and mass murders, could mean very little to an eternal being. They are but tiny blips on a timeline that constantly swings between good and evil."

My head popped up. I think it was the crowd's shuffling that woke me. I don't think they were necessarily agreeing with Reverend Emily. People were so much more comfortable when religion said, 'Do this,' 'Don't do that." None of us wanted to contemplate a Supreme Being who might be numb or even revel in the horrors of humanity. I mean, personally I didn't care much for the stern disciplinarian with the white beard who most people seemed to believe in. If you asked me he was overly concerned that people believe in him. As though he was some kind of narcissistic Peter Pan who needed people to believe in him in order to exist.

Then, Reverend Emily changed direction. "But you didn't come here for a sermon. You came to celebrate your friend, Curtis Barry. C.B., as we called him. For me, C.B. was a wonderful presence. Kind, industrious, thoughtful. I was personally thrilled with the things he was doing with Best Lives. It's always been an important group, one that our church is proud to support. C.B. was making it much stronger, much more important to people's lives. One of the things that always struck me about C.B. was the way he managed to live life to the fullest even in the face of death. Of course, we had no idea his death would come so quickly. Nor did we think of the irony, I suppose you'd call it, of his not dying of AIDS."

She let that sit. She was right. It was weird that he hadn't died of AIDS as he thought he would. As many of us thought we would. And it was ironic that he'd spent so much time trying not to die of AIDS, that he'd completely forgotten to protect himself from other more prosaic dangers like murder.

Self-consciously, I glanced back at Javier and Wellesley. Javier was listening to the reverend intently, while Wellesley's eyes were glued on—me. When I noticed that I spun my head around. Reverend Emily was saying, "I'm sure many of you would like to share stories about our friend, C.B. I'd like to start with someone who's been a tremendous support to all of us this week, Steve Meier."

Steve got up from where he was sitting with Erin and walked to the front of the room. He wore a black suit, a bit out of style, but that apparently didn't bother him as it had me. He seemed to trip on something as he walked to the front of the room. Glancing over his shoulder he saw nothing was there. By the time he reached his destination he was laughing at himself.

"If that was C.B.'s ghost, that would be the second time he's tripped me. The first was an accident."

He went on to tell a long and kind of pointless story about working with C.B. in the office one day and how he'd accidentally tripped on C.B.'s foot and they'd both had a big laugh about it. Honestly, it didn't sound that much like C.B. It could have been any polite person.

Finally he was done, saying, "I want to thank everyone for how nice they've been to me this week. The support you've given me assuming C.B.'s duties has been so appreciated. I only hope that I can continue to be of service to everyone. Thank you."

He cleared his throat. "I would like to ask Noah Valentine, who was with C.B. when he passed, to come up and say a few words."

My face turned beet red. I wanted to say no. I wanted to say I couldn't say anything, but everyone was looking at me. I couldn't believe Steve had said I was "with C.B. when he passed" like he just died of cancer in a hospital instead of being killed while I slept.

Numbly, I got up and walked to the front of the room. I had no idea what to say. I didn't want to tell a funny little story about C.B., I hadn't known him long enough to have one at hand. Not to mention, the only thing I'd been thinking about for the last five days was who might have killed him. And then I found myself talking about exactly that.

"As you all know, C.B. was murdered during the night at my apartment. At first, I wondered if it might have been someone here who killed him."

The crowd shuffled a little bit.

"But yesterday, a friend and I went to the advertising firm that C.B. used to work at, Imagination Station. We talked with his former employer. She told us that C.B. had not been as beloved there as he was here, but instead had managed to make a number of enemies. I think, and he may have mentioned this to many of you, he had a drug problem during that time which was the root of his difficulties. Anyway, his former employer thought it quite possible that someone from Imagination Station may have killed him. In fact, she called to tell me the name of C.B.'s killer but was attacked before she could."

At this point I looked directly at Detective Wellesley.

"That woman is still unconscious. But when she wakes up, she'll be able to tell us who C.B.'s killer was."

Abruptly, Eduardo began coughing and got up to leave the room. I stopped, not sure what to say for a moment. Why had he done that? Was he sick? Or had what I said upset him?

"I know this wasn't a funny little story about our friend, but I thought it was important to let you all know that the police are close to solving C.B.'s murder. Thank you."

I went back to my seat. Steve quickly took my place and asked, "Who would like to speak next? Perhaps something a little lighter?"

Bartholomew got up and began speaking. Even though I wasn't really listening I could tell that the story he was telling seemed to be more about him than C.B.

Louis leaned over Marc and whispered to me, "Was that strategic?"

"What do you mean?"

"If C.B.'s killer is here you just told him he's about to be caught."

"But he's not here. I mean, C.B. would have recognized him. And everyone here—"

"Do you know everyone in the room?"

I sat up straighter and looked around. No, I didn't know everyone in the room. In fact, there were a lot of people there I didn't know. They might not even be people who came to Best Lives.

"Oh, shit," I said.

People spoke for another forty-five minutes. Very few of the stories were funny or poignant or even important. Mostly I wondered why people had gotten up to share them. But, it all seemed to make people feel better. There were more smiles afterward than there were before.

The memorial was followed by fellowship. Many people left, but there were still a good twenty or twenty-five people remaining in the lobby for lemonade and cookies. Once we got out there, Leon hurried over to us.

"Where were you?" I asked.

"I was in the third row with Eduardo. You looked right at me several times."

"I did?"

"Don't even try to damage my ego by making me feel invisible."

"I wouldn't dream of it." Honestly, I hadn't noticed him. I had been kind of nervous while I stood in front of everyone.

"How's Eduardo?" Louis asked. "He had a funny cough."

"I don't know. He didn't come back. And I don't see him anywhere." Leon took his insanely expensive mobile phone out of his jacket pocket and dialed. "I'm guessing he went home."

We waited while the phone rang on Eduardo's end. It was picked up. Leon looked up at us and said, "Answering machine." After a moment he began leaving a message in Spanish.

"Do you see anyone who could be Daddy?' Louis asked me. I scanned the lobby in time to see Javier coming toward me with Wellesley on his heels.

"What are you doing here? I told you—"

"He was a friend of mine."

"That was an interesting stunt you just pulled," Wellesley

said. "But it's not going to work. I know you're behind all of this. You must think I'm an idiot. You expect me to believe that you slept through a murder and then you're coincidentally visiting a woman right before she's attacked. And now you want me to believe that some long-lost enemy from years ago is behind it. No. You're going down for this."

I was tempted to take the Taser out of my pocket and give her a good zap but fortunately she stormed off. So instead I looked at Javier and said, "How do you work with her?"

The look on his face told me I'd crossed some kind of cop line. "She *is* being logical. You do look suspicious and you've made yourself look even more suspicious."

"You believe me, though, don't you?"

"Yes, but then I know you took a sleeping pill so your sleeping through the murder makes sense."

"I should have told her about that, shouldn't I?"

"Probably. Maybe. I'm not—"

"But she would have arrested me," I reminded him. It had seemed like a good idea at the time.

"That's true. She would have. But you would have gotten probation."

"And a mountain of legal bills," Louis added.

"Also true. But it would have been better than a murder charge." He looked very unhappy for a moment. "I don't know if I'm going to be able to stop her from charging you."

"But—"

"Who are *you?*" Bartholomew said as he joined us, his eyes stripping off every stitch of Javier's clothing.

We introduced them and Bartholomew said, "So, you're investigating C.B.'s death? You haven't interviewed me yet. We really should set up a time for an in-depth interview."

Javier frowned at him. I'm sure he knew that people who volunteered to be interviewed often had nothing to contribute. It was certainly true of Bartholomew.

He began to ask Javier some very personal questions, like did he wear a gun in bed and had he ever arrested anyone in the nude. I glanced across the room and noticed Steve Meier chatting with a still grumpy Wellesley. Well, he would, wouldn't he? She was important, so talking to her made Steve important by association.

At that point, Louis interrupted and said, "All right. I've had enough lemonade. I think it's time we go have a drink."

14

By the time we got across town to New York, New York, happy hour had died down. Most of the Friday night crowd had wandered off to other bars or gone home to take a disco nap so they could get up around eleven and go back out.

As we walked into the bar, I said, "I can't stay out late. I have to work tomorrow."

"Your store doesn't open until eleven," Marc said.

"Yes, but I have to be there at ten," I said. And that was true, though Mikey could easily open without me. Actually, I probably didn't need to go in until afternoon, but work was still a good excuse not to get too drunk.

We walked over to the bar and Louis ordered two Stolis with soda water and a margarita for me. As we waited, Mariah Carey promised she'd be there for us—which I doubted, but it was a nice sentiment. Leon had gone to check on Eduardo.

Once we got our drinks, we decided to lean up against the far wall, which had a drink rail about chest high. Marc set his drink down on it and lit a cigarette.

"Well," said Louis. "I think it's safe to say Detective Wellesley isn't going to be much help."

"And it doesn't seem like Javier will be helping much either," Marc answered. "Did you invite him to come with us, by the way?"

"Oh, please tell me you didn't," I said.

"He had to go back to the station. Are you two not getting along?"

"It's complicated."

"It's only fun if it's complicated," Marc said, though I didn't think he believed that. He and Louis never seemed complicated.

"I really hope Julie Winters wakes up soon," I said. "And not just because I need her to save my ass. I mean, I hope she's gonna be okay."

"We should send flowers. If she wakes up," Marc said.

"We need to find the file with all the people C.B. fired," Louis said. "Do you think we should…"

"Should what?" I asked, suspicious of what might come next.

"Well, it's too bad your mother isn't here. We could just break in."

"No, we couldn't," I said. "And besides, the killer took the file. Javier told me this afternoon."

"He did?"

I nodded.

"Well, there has to be other information in there," Louis said. I think he was just in the mood for burglary.

"Which the Santa Monica police probably have," I pointed out. "On Monday we can talk to the other employees. Maybe someone remembers C.B."

"Oh, all right," Louis gave in. "Let's just hope you don't get arrested before then."

"Is there another way we can figure this out?" Marc asked. "What do we know about the killer?"

"He worked at Imagination Station with C.B.," I said.

"Well, we don't really know that. We think that," he corrected. "Stick to facts."

"The same person who killed C.B. attacked Julie Winters," Louis said.

"That's a supposition—"

"I knew you were going to say that. Let's accept that as a fact since it would be very strange if it's not the same person."

"Okay."

"He's been following me," I pointed out.

Louis nodded. "You saw him. That's a fact. And it must be how he knew you talked to Julie Winters."

"Did he follow you today?" Marc asked.

"I don't know. I mean, I don't think so. I was at Pinx all day so I didn't really go anywhere."

"So he could still be following you?" Marc asked.

"I guess he could be."

Why hadn't I worried more about his following me? He could have been sitting outside Pinx all day and I didn't check once. I felt safe in my store. That was probably why I hadn't been more diligent.

"He could be following you right now," Louis said.

"Or he could be in here," Marc agreed, "couldn't he?"

"Oh my God, don't even say that," I said, looking around the bar. I might have seen a couple of the regulars a few times, but for the most part I hadn't seen any of these people before. He could have been there. He could have been any one of them.

"I think it's more likely he was at the memorial," Louis said. "That would have been worth his while. Watching us drink isn't that valuable."

"Did you notice anyone suspicious at the church?" Marc asked.

"No," I said quickly, because I hadn't noticed anyone suspicious.

"We should go on a bar crawl," Louis said.

"Oh dear, you're in that mood."

"If this person is following Noah then let him follow us," Louis explained, then to me he said, "Cruise everyone in the bar."

"What? No. This is another plot, isn't it?"

"Come on, take a good look at everyone in here. Then we'll finish our drinks and go on to Detour. We'll have a drink there and see if any of these people show up."

"But Louis, it wouldn't be *that* surprising if some of these guys went on to Detour."

"And then we'll go on to The Gauntlet and see if that person follows us."

"What if he isn't actually coming into the bar?" I suggested. "What if he's out in his car?"

"Don't worry, we'll be cruising the parking lots too."

"Okay, could you use a different word? We're not actually going to cruise parking lots."

"Stake out?" he suggested.

"Never mind."

A bit later on we left and drove to Detour, which was just blocks from our building. It was a square, cement block building that had been painted black. There was a small parking lot attached. When we got out of the car, Louis told me to look around for the little gray station wagon that had followed me.

"He's following us," I pointed out. "So he's not here before we are."

As we got close to the bar's door—covered by thick strips of rubber than you had to push aside—Louis said, "Let's stay here a minute. Marc, light up a cigarette."

"Louis, I can smoke in the bar. They haven't made *that* illegal yet." It wasn't legal to smoke at work anymore and hadn't been for years. Which meant Marc went outside several times a day—I could see why he might not want to do it in his free time.

"If you're having a cigarette we won't look so weird staring at the parking lot."

"I suppose that's true," Marc said, grumpily getting out his cigarettes. He lit up and as he exhaled he scanned the parking lot. It looked very quiet. "Nothing's happening, can we go inside?"

"Just wait a couple of minutes."

We watched the traffic go by on Sunset. It occurred to me that we were playing a game of cat and mouse, except we didn't know what the mouse looked like or even if it existed. Then I wondered, who was the cat and who was the mouse.

A few minutes later we were inside having a drink, eyeing everyone who came inside. We didn't see anyone suspicious. I did see several guys I recognized, but I was pretty sure I only recognized them because they came into Pinx.

"Why?" Marc asked abruptly. "Why do you think the killer is following you?"

"Because I saw him," I said, not sure what I was being asked.

"Maybe he's not following you. I mean, why would he? What's he trying to do?"

"But he—" I started then decided I'd better play along. "Well, I guess he's trying not to get caught. And he wants to make sure I don't figure out who he is."

"All right," Marc continued. "We know he probably followed C.B. looking for an opportunity to murder him. We know he followed you yesterday morning. But we don't know whether he was trying to scare you or kill you. And then he followed us to Santa Monica."

"Uh-huh," I said.

"We don't know if he followed you on Tuesday and Wednesday—do we?"

"I don't remember noticing anything," I said, then tried to think back to make sure I was right. "Tuesday I was at Pinx all day. I mean, he could have been sitting outside in his car. He could have come in and rented videos. I wouldn't know."

"You wouldn't know if he's not one of the people we've met," Marc pointed out.

"True, but I was in my office a lot of the time. Mikey could have checked him out."

"If we know him, he probably wouldn't have risked coming in," Louis said.

"Except, I wouldn't have thought anything of it. Most of the guys at Best Lives rent from me."

"What about Wednesday?" Marc asked.

"IKEA during the day and Best Lives at night. I didn't notice anyone, so that—wait a minute. There was about twenty minutes when I was downstairs on the street. We unloaded my car and then I took two trips upstairs, once with Robert and once with Javier. I'm fairly certain I would have noticed someone."

"So, it's possible you weren't being followed on Wednesday?"

"Probably not. Is that important?"

Marc shrugged. "I don't know."

"Whoever it is, they don't have a lot of commitments. It seems to be pretty easy for them to spend time following you around," Louis said.

We grew quiet and looked around the bar. We finished our drinks and since nothing seemed to be happening at Detour we moved on. By the time we got to The Gauntlet it was our fourth bar, since we'd stopped briefly at the Faultline.

Louis switched to Calistoga. I'd switched to a Miller Lite and a shot of tequila after Detour because you don't order a margarita in a leather bar. I didn't hear what Marc ordered because I was distracted by the wet underwear contest that was happening on a six foot high platform on one side of the bar underneath a banner for Absolut vodka. There were some empty stools at the far end of the bar, away from the show. I was drunk enough to be annoyed by that.

The bartender brought our drinks over. Louis seemed to know him because he said, "Dom, this is our friend Noah."

Dom nodded at me. He was a tall guy, somewhere in his forties with curly salt-and-pepper hair and an out-of-date mustache. He looked familiar and, just as I nodded back, I realized I'd made out with him once at Cuffs the year before. I blushed.

"We're being followed," Louis told him. Although, since this was our fourth bar and we hadn't figured out who was following us or how they were following us it seemed like we probably weren't being followed.

"Yeah? Who's following you?"

"A murderer."

"So you thought you'd have them follow you here? You trying to class up the joint?"

"We're not sure if he actually comes into the bar. He might just be in a car outdoors," Louis explained.

"Who got murdered?"

"C.B.; Curtis Barry."

"Yeah, I knew him. He had a nice pair of assless chaps."

"He had a regular *friend*," Louis said, putting friend in air quotes. "All we know is that he called the guy Daddy."

Dom gave us a dubious look. "That doesn't make things any easier. Half the guys in here ask to be called Daddy."

"I know," Louis said. "Did you ever see C.B. with anyone he might have called Daddy? Older, bigger, something..."

"No. He always seemed to chase after the young ones. Daddy must have been saved for special occasions."

"Louis, the guy over by the shoeshine stand, he was in Detour," Marc said. "I think."

We all peered at him, including Dom. He was tall and blond, with a neck that stretched out and reminded me of Ichabod Crane. His eyes were glued to the heavyset MC as he poured a glass of water on a young guy wearing only a pair of BVDs. If this guy was following us, he was easily distracted.

There were two bartenders and not a lot going on because of the show. Dom seemed content to light a cigarette and stand near us.

"It's not fun being followed," Dom said, as though it had happened to him. "Kind of ruins your day."

"So does waking up with a corpse," I blurted.

Dom smirked and said, "Yeah, I can see where that might be a downer."

We'd now reached the part of the show where the MC held his hands over each contestant's head and we were supposed to applaud the one we liked. The guy from Detour seemed really into one guy, applauding and whistling. They must have been friends. Or something.

I turned my attention back to the bar. "You're moving down to Long Beach?" Louis said. "That's quite a hike."

"I'll probably get a job down there, eventually."

"Must be some guy."

Dom shrugged. "We bought a house."

"I want a house," Marc said.

"Not in Long Beach," Louis said, laying down the law.

"Well, no. Not in Long Beach. You're commuting?"

"At three in the morning it's only half an hour," Dom pointed out.

"Yeah, I don't think my boss would let me work your hours," Louis said.

Something, or rather someone, caught my eye and I realized I was looking at Javier. I got up and walked around the bar to him.

"What are you doing here?"

"Looking for you."

"How did you find us?"

"I drove around until I saw Marc's car."

I decided not to ask if that called for a license plate check or not. Nor did I mention how disconcerting it was. If he could find us easily, so could the killer.

"I got a call from Santa Monica. Julie Winters has woken up."

"That's great. Did she say who attacked her?"

"No. Her head injury was bad enough that it knocked out her short-term memory. She doesn't remember anything about the attack. Or you, for that matter."

"So she doesn't remember who might have killed C.B."

"She didn't remember C.B. was dead."

"But if she thought of someone who might have killed C.B. once, she could do it again."

"Right now she's recuperating. It could be a while."

"Are you going to get the list of people he fired?"

"Monday."

"Well, thank you, I appreciate your letting me know."

He reached out and with one finger lifted the flap on my breast pocket to look at the Taser in my pocket. For a moment I had the sick feeling you had to have a license to carry a Taser just like you did a gun.

"Is it illegal to carry a Taser?" I asked.

"That's not a Taser. That's a stun gun."

"There's a difference?" I asked. I'd been walking around calling it a Taser. Since, well, since I got it.

"A Taser is shaped like a gun and shoots darts at a suspect and shocks them. You can also shock them close rang. A stun gun is shaped like a deck of cards and only shocks close range."

"Okay, is it illegal to carry a stun gun?"

"No. It's not very smart though."

"Why? Why isn't it smart?"

"Well, just like a handgun, the chances of its being taken away from you and used against you are very, very high."

"But it's not illegal?" I repeated.

"No. Do yourself a favor though and start leaving it in your apartment."

Self-consciously, I flipped down the flap on my pocket. I wasn't going to leave it, my T—stun gun, at home. That made no sense.

"Is that everything you wanted to tell me?" I asked.

He hesitated. From the look on his face, I could tell there was actually something he wanted to tell me. I braced myself.

"I um, I also, I think I've let my, um, friendship with you cloud my judgment. I never should have helped you hide those pills. I have to take responsibility for that."

"Thanks, but I'm beginning to think that if I *had* told Detective Wellesley about the pills she wouldn't have believed I'd actually taken them."

"We could have tested you. Those pills are detectable in your system for days."

I shrugged. "Then she would have said I took the pills the night before so it would look like I was drugged while C.B. was being killed. She's not going believe me. It doesn't matter what the facts are."

"You might be right."

15

Knocking. Light. Pain.

Someone was pounding on my front door. Or maybe it was my head that was pounding. Cracking an eye open to look at the clock, pain grabbed my skull like a boney hand. It was only 8:13. I made a huge effort and sat on the edge of my bed trying to remember how many drinks I'd had. One each at Detour, the Faultline and New York, New York. Two at the Gauntlet. No, three. Then we went on to Cuffs and from there I didn't remember.

More knocking. Goddamn them.

"Coming!" I called out. I looked down myself. I wore only a pair of Calvin Klein boxer briefs. I got up and dug through a drawer until I found a pair of gray sweats and a T-Shirt that said, "That's Kathy!" Marc gave it to me—it was for an afternoon talk show staring an Olympic ice skater who was too chatty for sports commentary and not quite chatty enough for afternoon television. It failed.

Just like we'd failed to catch the killer the night before. All we'd caught were hangovers. With nothing on my mind other than how desperately I needed a glass of water, I went and opened the front door. Javier stood there in a pair of jeans that had probably come right off the shelf yet still looked perfectly tailored. With them, he wore a navy blue LOS ANGELES

POLICE ACADEMY T-shirt and a leather bomber jacket. He looked really good.

"Wow," he said. "You look bad."

"Why are you here?"

"You told me to come by and get the fingerprints you guys collected."

"Oh that's right. Come on in."

He stepped into my apartment and, when I didn't move, stood there with a stiff look on his face.

"Well?"

I couldn't tell if he was being an asshole or if my hangover was making me think he was being an asshole. Either way, I stormed over to my kitchen counter and picked up the samples we'd collected in their labeled plastic bags.

When I came back, he took them from me with a cursory glance. Then he gave me a terse, "Thanks."

Before he could get out of the door, I said, "Are you mad at me?"

"No."

"Then why are you being such a jerk? I mean, I just saw you a few hours ago and you were fine. I don't get it."

He stared at me for a little while—actually, a long while. And finally he exhaled heavily and said, "My T.O. heard a rumor that Wellesley is going to report me for having a relationship with a murder suspect."

"You mean me?" I really hated that murder suspect and me were synonymous.

He nodded. "Yeah. You. My two other cases are a seventy-six-year-old woman who probably poisoned her husband, and a pimp who beat one of his hookers to death."

He was right. That left me.

"What's a T.O.?"

"Training officer. He kind of still watches out for me."

"So, Wellesley knows you're gay?"

"Not exactly. She knows I'm friendly with you guys. She knows you guys are gay. She put two and two together."

"I'm sorry," I said, thinking that this was about the only thing Wellesley had ever correctly detected. At least to my knowledge. I'm sure she wouldn't have made it to detective without having done something or other right at some point. I just couldn't see it.

"Why does she hate me so much?"

"Well, there is something…"

"What?"

"It's not for me to say."

"She's going to tell people you're involved with me even though you're not."

He thought about that for a moment, then shrugged, looked at me and said, "She's divorced."

"Okay. What does that have to do—?"

"Her husband was gay."

"Oh. Well, that's not my fault," I said, and it certainly wasn't. In some ways it wasn't even her husband's fault. I mean, sometimes it seems like the entire world is telling you you're just going through a phase and maybe you should try even though it isn't at all what you want. Or just pretend, pretend to be someone you're not.

I mean, it's not okay that her husband lied to her, putting aside her feelings and dreams and hopes. It's also not okay that the world didn't care about that either. Whatever or whoever made him feel that he should marry a woman, well, they deserve a lot of the blame.

My guess was Wellesley wouldn't agree with that. She was angry at her husband and in turn every other gay man in the world. That was a lot of anger; anger focused directly at me.

"No, it's not your fault," Javier said. "It's not mine either."

"We need to figure out who killed C.B. soon, don't we?" I said.

"No. *I* need to figure it out."

I frowned. He frowned back at me.

"I'm going over to sit down with the guys in Santa Monica. I want to see what they have."

My phone started to ring.

"Go ahead and get that. I've got to get going," Javier said, picking up the plastic bags. "I'll get these processed."

He nodded at me and was gone. I went and picked up my cordless phone.

"I was thinking, have you learned much about your friend's family? I mean, if there's money there it might be worth looking into."

"Hi Mom," I said. My head was still pounding; the rhythm reminded me of the music from the night before. Bad techno that never seemed to end. I went into the kitchen and poured myself a glass of water from the tap.

"Well what do you think, dear? About your friend's family?"

"It doesn't matter anymore. The person who killed C.B. used to work for him at an advertising agency in Santa Monica. C.B. fired them."

I began drinking my water.

"I'm confused," my mother said. "Has the killer been caught?"

Taking a final big gulp, I put the glass back under the tap as I said, "Not yet. But we know it's someone who worked at Imagination Station, that's the ad agency. C.B. was kind of crazy when he worked there. He fired a lot of people."

"When did he work there?"

"A couple of years ago."

Carrying my water, I walked through the living room, through the bedroom and into the bathroom. I opened the medicine cabinet.

"That's a long time to hold a grudge," my mother pointed out.

"I know, but what if it was your dream job and your life just never recovered?"

"Oh you shouldn't ask me," she demurred. "I wouldn't kill someone even if they deserved it."

Setting the glass of water on the sink, I pulled a bottle of aspirin out of the medicine cabinet, shook out two and popped them into my mouth.

"If it turns out you're wrong you might want to look at his

family. Cotton was telling me about this divorce he did. He was sure the husband was going to kill his client." She stopped dramatically, "Noah, you don't think the killer will try to hurt you, do you?"

After I swallowed, I said, "No, like I said, it's definitely someone from the ad agency. The police are looking at former employees. The woman he worked for was attacked on Thursday night. She has a bad head injury. Can't remember a thing."

"And you don't think he'll attack you?"

I realized I wasn't being very reassuring, so I said, "If he's smart he's in Tijuana by now."

"But they're not smart," she said. "I mean, I know killers think they are, but they're not. You can't say it's smart to kill someone."

That was a funny idea. Were killers smart? This killer probably wasn't. First, C.B. had fired him, which meant he probably made some kind of mistake. Then, he'd left a fingerprint on my window. Of course, leaving me alive in the first place probably hadn't been very—

"Noah."

"What?"

"I asked if Javier had broken up with his boyfriend yet." She'd seen them together in November and had immediately decided it wouldn't work out.

"As a matter of fact, they have."

"You should do something about that. You're obviously ready to date again."

"You don't think the fact that my date died might have cooled my interest?"

"Well, it wasn't *your* fault. And it's very unlikely to happen again."

I wished I could be sure about that.

"I think Javier and I are just too different."

"Because he's Hispanic?"

"No. He's— he's not HIV-positive and that's just, I don't know—"

"You're afraid of infecting him? You'd use condoms, wouldn't—"

"Could we not be quite that specific?"

"Noah, a condom is hardly—"

"Did you have conversations like this with your mother?"

"Goodness, no. Your grandmother did say a few things to me before I married your father. Very negative things about marital duty and suffering through it for the good of my family. I mean, honestly, when it turned out sex with your father was pleasant I wondered if he was doing it wrong."

"I didn't really need to know that."

"How did I raise such a prude?"

There was someone at the door, so I stepped over and opened it. Marc was standing there.

"Mom, Marc is here. I have to go."

"All right, tell him I said hello."

To Marc I said, "My mom says hi."

"Hello, Angie."

"Okay, I've got to go now. Bye-bye."

"Bye dear."

I clicked the phone off and set it onto the table. "My God, it's like Grand Central Station up here."

"Sorry, I just wondered if you'd heard from Leon."

"Um, no. He calls my mother more than he calls me. You want me to call her back?"

"No, no, it's just—I've been trying to call him since last night."

"Did you try his mobile phone?"

"Of course. He's not answering it."

"It's probably too expensive to answer."

"Well, he doesn't answer his other phone either."

"He's probably with Eduardo," I said.

"That's what I'm worried about."

"Because he's kind of a suspect?"

"Well, yeah."

Was Eduardo the killer? He did have that weird reaction while I was speaking at the memorial. Of course, that could have been a coincidence. But I did sort of remember him having something to do with advertising. Did he have a gray station wagon? Or access to one?

"So, if it is Eduardo, why is he bothering with Leon? I mean, you and I are the ones who went to see Julie Winters."

"Well, he couldn't seduce us." Marc said, and he was right, too. He went on, "We think he killed C.B. for revenge and attacked Julie to silence her. What would be the reason to kill Leon?"

"Because he could?"

"I'm going to go over to Leon's in a bit."

"I have to be at the store today. Call me when you find him."

We said goodbye and I went to get into the shower. It was almost nine. After I cleaned myself, wrestled with my hair for a bit, and downed another large glass of water with two more aspirins, I began to feel human. Well, subhuman. Still, a significant improvement.

I got to Pinx around ten with a cardboard carrier filled with two vanilla lattes and a couple of poppy seed muffins. I badly needed the caffeine and sugar.

The back door was unlocked, so I knew Mikey was already there before I got to the counter. That meant I didn't have to worry about turning off the alarm that I kind of, sort of, hated.

"Good morning," Mikey said when he saw me.

I unloaded a latte and muffin in front of him. He looked up at me suspiciously. "It's not my birthday."

"I just thought I'd be nice. And, also, could you stay a couple of extra hours? Just through the rush?"

"Yes! Oh my God, thank you. I need the extra hours. Randy's gotten it into his head he wants to have a commitment ceremony."

"Do *you* want a commitment ceremony?" I asked, taking a sip of my delicious coffee.

"That's a really complicated question. If it was legal, I think I'd marry Randy. But, it's not legal. And I can't make up my mind whether having a commitment ceremony is a revolutionary act that says 'Fuck you America we're going to get married anyway' or if it's simply accepting our second-class citizenship in a pale imitation of heterosexuality."

"Do you love Randy?" I asked.

"Of course I love Randy."

"Then maybe you should just marry him as best you can."

He gave me a confused look. "But we don't have to be married to love each other."

"No. But if he wants the ceremony maybe you should do it."

"Without considering the political ramifications?"

"Well, I think you've already considered them. Now you can put them aside and just be happy."

"Would you be a groomsman?"

"For which groom?"

"Me, stupid."

"Oh, um, yeah. Sure."

Terrified of what I'd just agreed to, I went back to my office. I took off my jean jacket, hung it on the back of my chair, took a sip of my latte, and put my head down on the desk.

When my phone buzzed, I had no idea what time it was. Before I picked it up I tried to focus so I didn't sound like I'd just been woken up. I picked up the phone and carefully said, "Hello."

"Noah, there's a friend of yours here. He wants to say hello."

"Okay, I'll be right out."

I wondered why Mikey hadn't said your friend so-and-so since he knew most of my friends. As I walked to the front, I tucked my cotton button down shirt back into my pants since it had crept out while I was snoring on my desk.

"There you are!" Bartholomew said, his smile big and toothy. "I just came in to pick up a video or two and I wanted to say hello!"

"Hi Bartholomew."

"So tell me, what's good?"

I hated when people asked me that. Good being such a relative word when it came to movies. I was always forced to play twenty questions.

"What kind of movies do you like?"

"Well, good ones."

"Name a couple of movies you think are good."

"I'd love to see *Single White Female*."

"That's a new release. It's probably checked out," I said, glancing over at Mikey who nodded agreement.

"You don't have an extra one behind the counter?"

"No. But if you like thrillers, we probably have *Wait Until Dark*."

"Is that new?"

"It's from the sixties. Audrey Hepburn."

"No, I don't watch black-and-white movies. What about that new Melanie Griffith movie."

"*A Stranger Among Us*?"

"No, that's not it."

It was, but I didn't bother correcting him. "You know, you really should just look around."

"If you want something creepy, I think we have *The Hand That Rocks the Cradle*," Mikey said. He was better at this than I was.

Bartholomew gasped. "Yes, I'll take that."

"I'll get it," Mikey said, coming out from behind the counter.

"So," Bartholomew said. "Have they caught the killer yet? You said they were close."

"They're looking closely at former employees of Imagination Station," I said. At least I hoped they were doing that.

"Talk about a Jekyll and Hyde. I just can't imagine there being people who hated C.B. I hope that woman wakes up soon and tells them who it is."

There was something about Bartholomew's pumping me for information that bothered me. So I decided not to mention that Julie Waters had woken up but without part of her memory. Which reminded me, I should send her flowers.

"It should be cleared up soon."

"Thank God. I just hate looking at all my friends and wondering, 'Are you the killer?' Reminds me of that children's book, *Are You My Mother?* I used to read it to my nephew. Terrible child. I can't wait until he's fully grown so I can actively loathe him. Anyway, you know the book I mean."

"We have it on video."

"Got it," Mikey said, coming back with the video box for *The Hand That Rocks the Cradle*. He went in the back room to get the actual video. That left me smiling at Bartholomew.

"So, you're not wearing your gloves," I noted.

"Oh, vanity." He held out his hands and said, "Age spots. Already. I'm barely forty."

"I thought you said neuropathy."

"Did I? Well, it is embarrassing to say age spots. Try it. You'll see what I mean."

I declined. Of course, he was much older than forty. He could have age spots *and* neuropathy. Which made me ask, "How's your health, Bartholomew? Didn't you talk about having night sweats?"

"Oh yes, those come and go. Like my T-cells." He sighed and said, "What can you do? I suppose we all have to die sometime."

That made me a bit more disposed to like him, I guess. I mean, he probably wasn't C.B.'s killer. Why would the killer come in to rent a video from me? No, he was just a lonely man in poor health looking to add a little excitement to his afternoon.

"Well, I'm going to wander off to the porno section. Unless you have something really yummy behind the counter."

"We don't keep videos behind the counter." Actually, some of my employees did, but I really did discourage it. "Do you want me to call you when they catch the killer?"

He gasped. "Would you? That would be fabulous."

16

I LET MIKEY GO HOME AT EIGHT O'CLOCK. WE WERE STILL busy but he'd been there long enough and I felt like keeping him any longer would be taking advantage. Things remained busy from eight to nine, but then fell off quickly. People didn't rent many movies after nine o'clock. Yes, they might be staying up later on Saturdays than normal, but not to watch movies.

Around ten, I called over to Marc and Louis' and asked about Leon. They still hadn't heard from him. Marc had gone over to his apartment around seven and he wasn't there. He'd left a note taped to the door.

"At what point do you think we should call Javier?" Marc asked.

"Oh God. If he's gone on some kind of sex vacation he'll be mad we interrupted him." Although, he might not be too angry about Javier interrupting him. "I don't know, maybe you should call Javier. Better safe than sorry, right?"

I told myself it was nothing, nothing but bad timing. Leon was fine wherever he was. I made a stack of the tapes I hadn't been able to check in because I'd been too busy checking people out. There were about twenty-eight tapes. Most of them were easy, but some were late so I had to decide whether to ding the customer for a late fee. I looked them up and if they hadn't been late before I didn't charge them. Most of the time I let late fees slide—unless Mikey was there and he'd insist.

The other thing that slowed me down was rewinding. Again, I had to decide whether to charge the customer a fine. It was good policy not to, I thought. People might get angry and stop renting from us. However, there was one woman who brought back three tapes, late, and none of them were rewound. I added those charges to her account.

I'd been at this long enough to know she'd claim to have no idea the tapes were late and hadn't been rewound. Sometimes it's worth the risk of losing someone's business. When people kept tapes out too long that meant they weren't being rented, which meant I was potentially losing money. Another consideration would be if it was a new release. Then it was apt to rent a lot more often, so I'd be more likely to charge the late fee.

It took the better part of the last two hours to get through the returns, partly because I kept getting interrupted and partly because several people came by with more returns—getting them back to me right under the wire.

All together I had twelve tapes that needed to be rewound. Under the counter, we had a special, black rewinder that rewound the tapes very quickly, each one taking just over a minute. After I locked the front door, I made a quick trip to the tiny lavatory next to my office, then came back to the counter and put *Wait Until Dark* into the video player. Since we, or rather I, had mentioned it earlier I kind of wanted to see it. I figured I'd watch a little bit of that while I rewound tapes.

In between tapes and peeks at the TV, I maneuvered through the computer's menu and ran the nightly report which would tell me how much cash we'd taken in and how much we'd made in credit card charges. Then I'd have to count the money in the drawer and add up our credit card receipts to make sure everything balanced.

Even with the movie playing—the beginning was a little slow, mainly concerning the pretty drug mule giving Efrem Zimbalist Jr. the heroin-filled doll at the airport—I stopped when I thought I heard someone open the back door. Or was that on the TV? It might be a customer. They never managed to read the sign which said EMPLOYEES ONLY.

I came out from behind the counter and walked toward the back.

"Hello? Hello?"

No one answered. For a moment, I thought maybe I hadn't heard anything at all, no less someone coming in. I turned back toward the counter, facing front, and that's when I noticed the little gray station wagon sitting in front of the store. It was the one that had followed me. I was sure. It stopped me short. Standing there, I broke out in goose bumps. He was in the store. I'd heard him come in.

He had to be standing in the short hallway to my office or in the tiny lavatory. What to do? I could try to run out the back door, but that meant I'd have to run right by him. I could grab my keys off the counter and try to unlock the chain on the front door and go out that way. But he'd probably hear what I was doing and stop me.

Maybe if I was very, very quiet... I took a few tentative steps toward the counter, but then, unexpectedly, I felt the cold chill of a gun pressed up to a spot behind my ear.

"Where do you think you're going?"

I recognized his voice. "Steve? Steve Meier, is that you?"

"You hadn't figured it out?"

"No. I hadn't."

My mouth was dry and my tongue felt like it stuck to everything it touched. I had the terrible feeling my life was about to end even sooner than I'd thought. On the TV, Audrey Hepburn was joking with Ephraim about what a good blind lady she was.

"You have an office back there, don't you?"

"Yes, I do."

"We're going back there."

He grabbed me by the arm and, while keeping the gun pressed against the back of my head, turned me around. I tried not to think about what was going to happen after Steve shot me. How upset my mother would be. The mess my financial information was in and that she'd have to deal with it. I really should have been more organized. Oh crap, I was thinking about what would happen after I died.

Steve opened the door to my office and pushed me in.

"Why, Steve? Why did you kill C.B.?"

"Curtis Barry ruined my life."

"You worked at Imagination Station and he fired you?"

"Yes. He ruined my life."

"But, how did you get—he didn't give you HIV, did he?"

"No. I'm not HIV positive. That was a ruse."

"Oh." For some reason that made things even worse. He'd lied. He'd lied to all of us. He'd stolen whatever life C.B. had left and now he was going to do the same to me. And then, then he'd go on and live as long as—

"Sit behind the desk."

I sat. A random thought flew across my mind—I had to keep him talking. It was the only way I'd survive. I had to keep him talking until I figured out what to do.

"I, uh, I don't understand. If you knew C.B. why didn't he know you?"

"He ruined my life."

"You said that."

"After he fired me, I went to see a lawyer. I wanted to sue him, but I couldn't. He held all the cards. California is an at-will state, my lawyer said. Employers can fire people for any reason. There was nothing I could do."

"That's awful."

"It was my dream job. I'd always wanted to work in advertising ever since I was a child. It looked, it looked glamorous on TV—"

Oh my God, I thought, was he talking about *Bewitched*? Had Darren Stevens seduced him into advertising?

"After he fired me, I lost my apartment, I lost my fiancé, I lost everything. I didn't have another job for eighteen months, and that was in insurance. I don't care about insurance. It's boring."

He pushed the gun hard against my temple.

"I was writing an insurance policy for an actor who wanted to insure her ears, when it hit me. I had to make him pay. I had to ruin his life, just like he'd ruined mine. So I went looking for him. I found out he wasn't at Imagination Station anymore and then I found him at Best Lives."

Emotion seemed to overcome him for a moment, then he went on, "At first I thought he was getting what he deserved. AIDS. He'd ruined his own life, so I didn't have to. But I still wanted him to know. Wanted him to know I was glad his life was ruined. So I went to confront him and—he didn't have any idea who I was. Didn't know me at all. He started talking to me like I was one of you, like I was some filthy fag with a disease. He'd ruined my life and he didn't even remember me. That was almost as bad as his firing me. He ruined my life and didn't even have the courtesy to remember my name. That's when I knew I was going to kill him."

"That's a terrible story," I said. "C.B. should have remembered you."

"Thank you. It's kind of you to say. Now take out a piece of paper and a pen," he said. That's when I knew where this was going. He was going to make me write a suicide note.

I did as I was told, taking a piece of Xerox paper out of one drawer and a fine point marker out of another. Even though I'm right-handed, I put the pen in my left hand.

"Write 'I killed C.B.'"

I positioned my hand but stopped before I wrote anything. "No greeting? No, 'to whom it may concern' or 'goodbye cruel world?'"

"No, just write what I said."

I rested my right hand in my lap for a moment. "You want it to be believable, don't you?"

"It's in your handwriting."

"I would use a greeting." I slipped my right hand under my left arm, being as subtle as I could be. "And I wouldn't start with 'I killed C.B.' I would start by explaining. So, why did I kill C.B.?"

"Because he was an asshole who ruins people's lives."

"That's your reason for killing him. What's mine?"

I had my fingers on the left breast pocket of my jean jacket, hanging there on my chair. That was the pocket that held my Taser—er, stun gun.

"Stop it. I'm the one with the gun. You do what I say."

"That reminds me, where did I get the gun?"

"What?"

I began teasing the stun gun out of my pocket.

"If I'm killing myself, where did I get the gun?"

"You stole it."

"Who did I steal it from?"

"Erin."

"Your drug-addicted girlfriend has a gun?"

I now had the stun gun all the way out of my pocket. I felt around for the safety and clicked it off.

"You don't meet the best class of people when you do drugs, okay?" Steve said.

I almost asked him how I'd know where she lived, but then I remembered she rented videos from me. "How did I know she had a gun?" That was a better question.

"She mentioned it at the dinner party."

"Except she didn't."

"No one will remember that she didn't."

"My friends will, she will."

"I'll remember that she did."

"So, I broke into her apartment and stole a gun so I could kill myself? That doesn't make—"

I threw my left arm up, knocking Steve's arm away so that now Erin's gun was pointed at the ceiling. I drove the stun gun into his crotch and zapped him. Steve screamed. The gun went off with an incredible bang. I kept jamming the stun gun into his crotch until the gun fell out of his hand.

I heard someone rushing in the back door and a moment later, I was looking at Javier. "It's Steve Meier. He did it. He wanted me to write a confession and then he was going to make it look like I killed myself."

Javier stepped over Steve and picked up his gun. With a deft move, he unloaded it. Then he picked Steve up off the floor and arrested him.

"Call 911 and get backup," he told me.

So I did.

17

"WHAT WERE YOU DOING AT PINX VIDEO?" LOUIS ASKED Javier as he set his special breakfast quiche onto the table.

Javier seemed to blush a bit. I was still bleary-eyed. We'd been up until about three dealing with Steve Meier's arrest and my witness statement. He now faced one murder charge and two attempted murder charges.

"Actually, I was there to arrest Noah. Brenda, Detective Wellesley, was planning to arrest him this morning. I thought he might prefer to have me arrest him.

"Well, that was thoughtful of you," Marc said.

"I'll say," Leon said. "Were you planning to do a strip search?"

Now Javier really did blush.

Louis was passing out pieces of quiche. I took a sip of my mimosa. "Now, where were you yesterday?" I asked Leon.

He'd brought Eduardo with him so the answer was obvious. Still, I thought someone should ask.

"Let's just say I was indisposed."

Eduardo giggled. Then took out a tissue and blew his nose.

"I'm allergic to trees," he said. "It always starts in February. Pollen."

"Oh, that's why you left the memorial so abruptly," I said.

"Oh really Noah," Leon said. "You really didn't think—"

"I didn't know what to think. I'd said that Julie was going to wake up and tell us who the killer was and Eduardo started coughing. At the time it seemed like there might be a connection."

"No, it was just trees," Eduardo said, then as though to make his point he sneezed.

"Did you call your mother to let her know everything's fine?" Louis asked.

"I called her from the car," Leon said.

"You called my mother long distance with your expensive mobile phone?"

"I didn't say very much more than that we'd caught the killer and that you were fine."

"We? You didn't have anything to do with it."

"I was actively involved in flushing him out."

"You were actively involved in something," Louis said, making Eduardo giggle again.

I took my first bite of the quiche. It was yummy, but then I'd had it before. The fact that the crust was made of shredded potatoes and that Louis had also made blueberry banana muffins made me ask, "Are you still on *The Drinking Man's* diet?"

"I don't think so," Louis said. "They should rename it *The Sloppy Drunk Diet*, because that's what you end up being."

"Hear, hear," Marc said, sipping his drink. "Now, what about the gray wagon? Where did that come in?"

"His girlfriend, Erin," Javier said. "A Renault Sportwagon from 1982."

"Oh. I would never have known that," I said. "I'm a little vague on the difference between a Chevrolet and a Buick. I know even less about French cars."

I glanced at Javier, but he looked away. We were talking but not talking. He seemed to be clinging to the group. I wanted to get him alone and ask whether the rumor he'd heard about Brenda had come true. Had she gotten him in trouble or not?

"How is Detective Wellesley taking it?" I nudged.

"Well, I'd say she's having a bad day. I called her a couple of hours ago. She's still trying to think of a way to arrest you for something."

Which made me think it might have been a really good idea to hide my mother's pills from her. In fact, it might be a good idea to hide all future criminal activity from Wellesley. Not that I was planning any…but, hey, you never know.

"This should teach you all a lesson," Javier said.

"Don't sleep with the window open?" Leon guessed.

"No. One of the reasons Steve killed C.B. here is that he knew a little bit about Noah. He knew that Noah had been involved with murders before and that he would be looked at closely."

Suddenly, the quiche wasn't sitting well.

"This really needs to be the last time," Javier said. "You're putting yourselves in too much danger."

"To be fair," I said. "I didn't plan any of this. It was kind of thrust on me. So to speak."

"I know. But, in the future. You need to stay out of these things."

"I think I'd be perfectly happy if no one within a three-mile radius of me ever died again," I said truthfully.

Javier sat back, seeming almost satisfied by that. I mean, he had to understand that I didn't go around looking for these things, right?

"I had some good news," Marc said. "My boss called me yesterday. Apparently, my one-third of a temp secretary went to her and accused me of conducting 'homosexual' business in the office, whatever that means. She's being reassigned on Monday."

"Good for you," I said.

"I told you he had his boss wrapped around his finger," Louis said.

"I do not!" he protested, before adding, "She does really like me though."

"Oh, I'm so sorry I can't join you for brunch," Patty Wong said. I jumped; so did Leon. None of us had seen her come up to us. "I have to go to church. None of you go to church, I see."

Indeed, she was dressed in a very elaborate pants suit, though she still smelled of drugstore cologne.

"You really should go. It is so good for the soul."

Louis said, "We were all in church Friday evening."

It took me a moment and then I realized, we were in church for C.B.'s memorial. Patty was making a sound akin to grumbling. She didn't enjoy her criticisms being rebuffed.

"Actually, I've been going every week," I said. It was true, in its way.

"Hmmmm," Patty nearly groaned. "I have to run. So sorry I couldn't join you. We'll get together another time, I'm sure. Bye Lee, you look so handsome today."

When she was far enough away, Javier asked, "Who was that?"

"Patty Wrong," Leon said.

"Wong," corrected Marc. "He always does that."

"Because she's wrong. She pretends to know me but she doesn't. And she acts like my name is Lee, which it most definitely is not."

After that, conversation drifted from the Grammys to the March on Washington which was two months away to Javier's family about whom we knew very little.

"They're just you're average Irish-Mexican family," he demurred.

"Catholic?" Louis asked.

"Very. What the Pope says goes."

Fortunately, everyone left him alone about that. From previous conversations, I knew that Marc and Louis weren't exactly fans of religion and I was, well, I wasn't either.

A bit later, Javier got up and said that he needed to get going. Not surprising since I think he'd gotten even less sleep than I had. I stood up too and asked, "Do you want me to walk you out?"

"Oh, um, no that's okay. You stay here with your friends."

"Okay. Well, um, thank you."

"For what? You kind of had things under control."

"For believing in me, I guess."

"Um, okay," he said, then waved at us and left.

"Well, what should we do this afternoon?" Marc asked.

"Beer bust at the Faultline?"

"Oh Louis, after Friday night how can you possibly—"

"We have plans," Leon said.

Eduardo giggled.

"How about a movie?" Marc suggested.

"I want to see *Army of Darkness*," Louis said.

"You can't be serious. How about *Aladdin*?"

Louis just raised an eyebrow.

A few days later, I had an appointment at Becker-Morse Medical Group located in Beverly Hills-adjacent. They were on the second floor of a pink granite office building. They didn't validate, so I hunted through the nearby residential neighborhood until I found a parking spot that was vaguely legal.

The waiting room was a discordant pink and blue. I sat down with the latest issue of *Time* magazine, which was all about the science of love. Women chose men with heavy beards and lots of testosterone at one time of the month and round-faced testosterone-challenged men at another. Making the correlation that heavy-bearded men were never faithful, while round-faced men were—something which I didn't find necessarily true. But it was apparently scientific.

It said something like this: "Women would fall in love for two years, but if the union didn't produce a baby by then, they'd drift until either they eventually got pregnant or moved on to another man for a better chance at conceiving. Each child born extended the established relationship. From an evolutionary standpoint it meant that, if necessary, women might look to bearded men to conceive but rely on round-faced men to help with child rearing."

Of course, it was all written from a very academic, straight perspective—and male, since it made women seem kind of awful. It didn't make any mention of how long a gay person might be in love or what kinds of faces attracted us. Personally, I tended toward the heavy-bearded guy. So, was that my evolutionary purpose? To see if I could distract Mr. Heavy-beard long enough to give Mr. Round-face a chance with the ladies?

The nurse was calling me. He was a stocky guy with a five o'clock shadow. And, yes, I thought he was kind of cute. His name was Gino and I was getting to know him for all the wrong reasons. On the way to the exam room he made me stand on the scale.

"Hmmmm," he said.

"What?"

"You gained two pounds. Keep it up."

"Okay."

"You're still underweight, so don't freak out."

"I wasn't. I mean, I don't really love being skinny." Or at least as skinny as I was.

"The grass is always greener."

He led me into the exam room, took my temperature, and checked my blood pressure. I appeared to be alive. That was good.

"Okay, well, the doctor's going to be a couple of minutes. You should have brought the magazine you were reading."

"That's fine. It wasn't that great an article."

Gino left me alone.

What would have been a great article about love? Telling me that love was basically an evolutionary function governed by hormones and monthly menstrual cycles wasn't all that helpful. Love was either the best thing in the world or the worst. And it could go from one to the other in a matter of minutes. How did you know when to say yes to it and when to say no.

Specifically, should I say yes to Javier if I got the chance? Would being with him be a disaster or would it be heaven? He seemed like a decent guy who wanted to do the right thing even when the right thing was against the rules. But what if that was just the way he seemed? What if he wasn't really that and I fell in love with him and later on found out—

No, that wasn't fair. My problems were not Javier's fault. My problems were mine. I'd picked Jeffer and Jeffer had turned out to be less than honest. Far less. I was not what you'd call a good judge of character, so just choosing Javier made me feel like there must be something very, very wrong with him. I just didn't know what it was yet. Well, maybe I did. He was kind of moody and not out at work or to his family and kind of freaked out by my being HIV positive.

Actually, it was stupid to even think about him. But I did. And, given the chance I would be willing to, I don't know, fall in love with him I guess. If he wanted that. I just didn't think—

My doctor, Doctor Sam—who I'd read was on some important AIDS commission for the whole state of California—came into the room. He was blond and very good-looking, the kind of guy you could put under the encyclopedia entry for DOCTOR and no one would complain. His perfect nose was buried in my thickening file.

"Hi, Noah. Tell me what's been going on?"

I nearly panicked. Did he know that I'd woken up with a dead man and then nearly been killed less than a week later?

"Um, nothing."

"Have you been under a lot of stress?"

"Maybe. Why?"

"Your T-cells have dipped more than I would expect."

"How much?"

"You're under 400."

"Is it permanent?"

"It may be, it may not be. That's why I asked about stress. Stress can negatively impact your immune system. What do you do to keep stress under control?"

That was a tough question. The honest answers were, 'Carry a stun gun' and 'Chase murders with my friends.' Neither of which was the answer my doctor was looking for. I stared at him blankly.

"You could take a yoga class."

Twisting myself into a pretzel sounded stressful. Still, I said. "Okay. I'll look into it."

"I could raise the dosage on your AZT. But I'd like to see

what you can do on your own. Regular meals, exercise, relaxation. No smoking, no alcohol, no recreational drugs."

"Um, okay."

"We'll check your numbers in two months and see where you are."

"Okay."

"This isn't the beginning of anything. All right?"

What did that mean? The beginning of what? Was he telling me—

"So, any questions, anything you need to ask me about?"

I shook my head.

"Okay then. Why don't you come back in eight weeks. The nurse will bring in the order for blood work and then you can make an appointment. And you're done for today."

"Okay."

He rested a hand on my shoulder for a moment and left the room. That brief gesture was almost more frightening than the phrase "the beginning of anything." Yes, he said it wasn't the beginning of anything, but I hadn't even thought—

It really felt like he'd meant it could be the beginning of my health declining but didn't want to say that, so he said it wasn't. But it could be. And that was scary.

A minute or so later, Gino came in and gave me the order for the blood work I'd get in two months, which would tell me whether or not this really was the beginning of something. I thanked him and got off the table. I walked out of the room right after him and went back to the front desk to make my next appointment.

Numbly, I drove home. I shouldn't take this too seriously. This was a long road. I knew that. Except, it wasn't always a long road. I could have ARC soon and after that—

I really shouldn't think about that. It wasn't happening yet and maybe, probably, wouldn't be happening for a long time. But it would happen. Someday. There had been more and more days when I was able to forget about that. Days when I felt like everyone else. "This isn't the beginning of anything" was a reminder that someday would happen eventually. It was just a matter of time.

When I walked into my apartment, I noticed there was a message on my answering machine. I walked over and hit the button. It was Javier.

"Listen, I think I'm ready to talk. I know I've been weird so maybe you don't want to. And you know, if you don't that's fine. I mean, it's not fine but I understand. I guess that's what I mean. So, call me. Or, don't. Up to you."

I erased the message.

LOUIS' BREAKFAST QUICHE

The thing about practically any recipe that uses a pie dish is that inevitably the ingredients are portioned for a pie pan you don't happen to have. So there are no amounts in this recipe. Simply adapt to your pan.

1. Lightly oil the pie pan.
2. Shred potatoes.
3. Spread them on the bottom of the pie pan and up the sides to form a "crust." After you're done spreading the "crust," it should be about as thick as a traditional crust.
4. Brush the "crust" with melted butter. Here you want to be careful that you haven't used too much oil in step one and you're not using too much butter. Too much of either and the potatoes will be soggy.
5. Bake in the oven at 375 degrees until it begins to brown. Allow to cool.
6. Cook some breakfast sausage. The better your sausage the better your quiche. If you use sausage links, slice them. You can use chorizo if you want to give the quiche a Mexican flare. When the sausage is fully cooked, put it into the "crust."
7. Add shredded cheese. Gruyere is the best choice for

cheese. Swiss is fine for everyday. Queso from the mercado if you're going Mexican. Avoid cheddar, as it doesn't come out well. Use a lot of cheese, but leave room for the custard.

8. Typically, custard is about 6-8 eggs, depending on whether you're using large, extra-large or jumbo. And about a cup or a cup-and-a-half of heavy cream. When you've mixed it all together it should be about the color of butter.

9. Add pepper and nutmeg to taste. I don't add salt. You can, but cheese is typically salty enough on its own.

10. If you'd like to add caramelized onions, spinach, mushrooms, broccoli or anything else you can think of, you should do so at this point—if there's room.

11. Add the custard mixture to the pie and bake at 375 degrees until the top is brown and the custard set.

ALSO BY MARSHALL THORNTON

IN THE BOYSTOWN MYSTERIES SERIES

The Boystown Prequels

(Little Boy Dead & Little Boy Afraid)

Boystown: Three Nick Nowak Mysteries

Boystown 2: Three More Nick Nowak Mysteries

Boystown 3: Two Nick Nowak Novellas

Boystown 4: A Time for Secrets

Boystown 5: Murder Book

Boystown 6: From the Ashes

Boystown 7: Bloodlines

Boystown 8: The Lies That Bind

Boystown 9: Lucky Days

Boystown 10: Gifts Given

Boystown 11: Heart's Desire

Boystown 12: Broken Cord

IN THE PINX VIDEO MYSTERIES SERIES

Night Drop

Hidden Treasures

Late Fees

OTHER BOOKS

The Perils of Praline

Desert Run

Full Release

The Ghost Slept Over

My Favorite Uncle

Femme

Praline Goes to Washington

Aunt Belle's Time Travel & Collectibles

Masc

Never Rest

ABOUT THE AUTHOR

Marshall Thornton writes two popular mystery series, the *Boys-town Mysteries* and the *Pinx Video Mysteries*. He has won the Lambda Award for Gay Mystery twice, once for each series. His romantic comedy, *Femme* was also a 2016 Lambda finalist for Best Gay Romance. Other books include *My Favorite Uncle*, *The Ghost Slept Over* and *Masc,* the sequel to *Femme.* He is a member of Mystery Writers of America.